Best James Aug! Please the typo

Agatha and Olivia

a novel by
James Antonio

PublishAmerica
Baltimore

First printing

Hardcover 978-1-4489-4528-3
Softcover 978-1-4512-5724-3
PUBLISHED BY PUBLISHAMERICA, LLLP
www.publishamerica.com
Baltimore

Printed in the United States of America

Chapter One

Agatha was on her way to work feeling quite unhappy. It was a Monday morning for one thing and it was November too. But that wasn't all. As she walked determinedly along she clutched her pathetic little brown purse as if it was all that remained between herself and utter starvation. Her lunch, a clump at the bottom of a plastic grocery bag, dangled precariously from her fingers. It seemed to her, awfully, like the weight of the whole world was on her shoulders. She passed a school, glancing briefly at the children frolicking around the desolate yard. She remembered with wistfulness when Tamara was just as young. She'd had plenty of hopes and dreams. She was madly in love and they were going to have a house of their own one day, she and Grant, and Tamara would be a star, a singer perhaps or an actress in the movies. But it was nothing like that. They were ordinary people having a humdrum sort of existence, struggling in many ways. Cars swished by drearily. It had rained hard overnight and into the morning and the asphalt glistened like slick under the heavy gray sky. She could see her breath, and the sweet scent of wood smoke was suggestive of winter. She knew the agreeable smell was coming from the nice new houses on the long straight street across from her apartment building that had opened where a woods used to be. She was reluctant to look that way anymore.

She was working a longer shift. She took all the hours she could get and Tamara and Grant would just have to fend for themselves for supper. Tamara was a good enough cook and she'd left a note on the counter listing all the things she could prepare. This way she didn't have to worry about Grant, who would probably come home after work because it was a Monday and he was likely broke.

She worked in the produce section of the supermarket. It was called Food Dreams and it was the only store in Awappich. Almost everybody seemed to go there and it did a thriving business, though she'd often hear the owner and his wife complaining about the expenses. From what she saw they didn't appear to be doing all that badly. The Mister drove a big new pickup or sometimes a sports car if the weather was nice and the Missus, a silver sedan that looked expensive. The boys, their sons, had nice cars too, new and sporty-looking, in bright colors. So it was hard for her to understand the complaints.

The first thing she did when she stepped into the store was sally to the back and put her lunch in the refrigerator. The lunch room was a well-lit and bright enough little place with a picnic table and framed pictures of perfect-looking meals on the walls. The pictures were losing their sharpness, faded over time, and more than once she'd hinted to Mr. And Mrs. Jardin that they ought to be replaced.

She wore an apron when she was at work, over the standard issue navy blue slacks and the shirt. She knew it made her look heavier than she was and as she padded her way through the store to Produce she could feel the ties tugging at the neck. In one way this was her favorite time of the day. The aisles were mostly deserted save for a few early risers and she could hear soft music piping through the sound system. It was a placid environment, and it was easier to work when there weren't any customers pecking away at things. She noticed that almost all of the oranges were gone. Three or four lay there like sad lost children. She made a mental note. It was the time of year when oranges were just starting to get good again, juicy and sweet. The grapefruit were mostly gone too and the few that remained had soft, gleaming yellow skins under the relentless fluorescent lights. By the time she was done with inventory she needed everything in varying quantities. The item that was hardest to sell was definitely watermelons. If the truth were known she hated the things. There they were in a rugged cardboard bin like big lazy green slugs. Who in their right darn mind, she wondered, ate watermelons at this time of the year? She glowered at them as if they were mischievous kids. Down near the bottom of the pile she glimpsed a splotch of wet and figured that one of them was cracked. She turned abruptly and was about to go to the walk-in cooler when she bumped into Nathan. He was the owners' oldest son, a handsome young man who strikingly resembled his mother. He was tall and black, with dark eyes and brows and a full head of hair cropped to a shadow.

"Hey, Aggy, what's up?"

"I didn't hear you," she told him. "It's those cool shoes you're wearing, they don't make any noise."

He looked her in the eye and as far as she was concerned he could continue doing so for the rest of the day.

"You like 'em, do you?"

"The color. They're different. How many people have red shoes? You can get away with that. Other men would maybe get odd looks."

"I bet you get plenty o' looks, Aggy." He chuckled and patted her shoulder. "I best let you ramble or we're not gonna get anythin' done."

Agatha peered down at her charm bracelet. She practically wore it all the time, except when she was in bed. She believed it would bring her good luck in a big way but it hadn't, at least not yet. The ace of hearts was staring her right in the face and, with a smile, she took it to mean that it was going to be a good day.

She went and got what she needed a few things at a time. She used a little trolley she pushed along and the wheels squeaked like chattering mice. As she stocked her displays, setting them up as appealing as could be, her mind was on Nathan. He flirted with her all the time. She liked him, there was no question about it, and knew, if she'd not been married, she would have yielded long ago. Still, the temptation remained and *he* just wouldn't let up. It was both exciting and scary all at the same time. Certainly she could use a little something in her life! Things with Grant weren't the best, yet she knew it wasn't entirely his fault.

It took her well over an hour to finish except for the cauliflour. She pushed the trolley to the back of the store enthusiastically, knowing a coffee break was in the offing, passing a handful of shoppers along the way. She knew a couple of them by name and said "Hi!" with a smile. She appreciated their paying her wages but she kind of sickened at times of seeing the same people and pretending she was glad. They might even sense her friendliness was but an act and the thought made her blush.

She left the trolley and stepped into the big walk-in refrigerator. The fans were buzzing madly and the frigid air blew right into her face, fluffing her long blond hair, which she had tied in a pony tail. She went over and lifted a flat of cauliflour off a pile by the wall and, carrying it out, met Nathan.

"I'll help you," he said, pulling the box out of her hands and shoving the heavy door closed with his foot.

They walked together to produce and, though she liked his company, she was concerned someone might get the wrong idea. "Thanks," she told him as he set the cauliflour on the floor.

"Hey, no problem, Aggy," he smiled. Her face reddened.

He walked away in his tight enough jeans and she watched him with her head lowered, peeping out from under her brows, pretending instead to be examining her miserable fingernails. In the lunch room she made herself a cup of instant coffee, which she was hardly fond of. She sat there with Harvey, the butcher. He was at least fifty, married with children, and seemed quite content with his lot in life. She could easily understand why. He had a nice newer home with a swimming pool and his wife worked in an office. They didn't, either of them as far as she knew, have any bad habits that might lead to financial ruin, ill health, or divorce. Their money all went on things necessary and reasonable. She winced when he mentioned they'd bought savings bonds. She and Grant never bought anything like that because there was rarely a cent left over after the bills were paid. At least Grant, with his profession, belonged to a good union and would get a nice pension. She, on the other hand, would not get a company pension at all. It was always upsetting to hear others going forward so. She wasn't jealous, but rather regretful.

"I worked on Saturday," she said, her hands embracing the cup. "But I was off yesterday. It was nice to be away. There's a lot to do at home. I guess you know. Nobody's ever really 'off'."

"You can say that again!" Harvey beamed. He nodded reflectively. "When we go away anywhere I feel like there's nothing to do but have a good time. The 'free as a bird' cliché! I like that. It's true too. All you have to do is get in your car and head on out....Go on a trip, you and Grant. Drive, fly, take a boat. Anything. But get the hell away! That's the secret."

"I'd like to," she said, gazing somewhat sadly at her reddish, chapped hands. "Grant's been getting a lot of work lately and so have I." She knew that their having to work was hardly the reason they hadn't gone anywhere on vacation. "Tamara can look after herself, I know that. I don't like to leave her alone for very long though. But a week away sure would be nice,"

The butcher sucked some coffee up from a great big mug and sighed with satisfaction. Harvey was a little gruff but she liked him. He just seemed to take life as it came along, one day at a time. It was admirable. When he left in a while he told her to have a good day. She smiled warmly.

Broccoli was the hot item at seventy-nine cents a bunch and she had trouble keeping up with the demand. Tomatoes, at sixty-nine a pound, were disappearing fast too. Many people stopped by just to take advantage of the specials, purchasing in large quantities without buying anything else. She could

understand it but found it irksome. Most of them looked like they hadn't missed a meal in their life and appeared well enough off, in good clothes, and drove away in newer cars. She attributed this mania to greed. Though she ferreted out bargains herself she at least had good reason.

She was summoned to take cash every once in a while and she loathed it. It had been fine in the past but was now frustrating what with the use of credit and debit cards and having to sell lottery tickets too. Whenever he could, Nathan came and helped her bag groceries which made things tolerable, and time went quickly by.

By the afternoon coffee break she noticed that her ace of hearts had turned around, offering only its cold, plain silver back. That meant her luck was going to change. She didn't have a coffee. Instead, she just sat there listening to a couple of the other girls blabbering away about frivolous and sundry things.

She thought she should have stayed out of the lunch room and wandered around produce instead but she was polite and smiled and, feigning interest, managed to nod now and again in amongst their rat tat tat of words. There were hair appointments, sales on panty hose, a filling at the dentist, someone's flat tire, and a leaky roof at an aunt's house.

"I saw hair spray on special," the strawberry blond chirped, "and I'm gonna go and buy a whole bunch. It's good, like, till forever."

They were lucky, Agatha mused. They lived at home with their parents and all their bills were paid for them. As a gesture of good will they might offer their mother or father a token amount for room and board which might even be refused. Oh, were they going to find out!

When she began sorting through the new lot of tomatoes she could see there'd be trouble. There were twenty cases on the pallet and, opening the one, she noticed that not only were many of them green, there was a nest of rotten ones at the bottom marinating in juice. The nest was large, a clutch of white fuzz like cotton batting, and the mess stank terribly. She felt slightly sick to her stomach. She set to work and, before long, had a full case of red tomatoes ready to be carried out for display. The rotten ones were at the bottom of the garbage can, wallowing in a putrid pool, some squished and mushy and unrecognizable and others split and caved in. She'd put the green ones in cases on another pallet to ripen, knowing that some of them, picked too soon and too green, would rot before turning red at all.

She had trouble with the broccoli too. It was harder to handle for one thing, the waxed cardboard cases often insecure, the bottoms dropping open suddenly. Broccoli was packed in crushed ice and the cold and wet chapped and cracked her skin. She dumped out a couple cases on the stainless counter and didn't like what she saw. Some of the crowns were mushy, others turning yellow and brown. She tugged the strong, stubborn elastics off the bunches and took apart the stocks, of which there were usually two or three to a bunch. She scrupulously examined the crowns to make sure they were green enough and then rebunched them, tossing out the bad. She placed the bunches carefully back in the boxes and wheeled out the whole lot to be put on display.

No sooner did she get over to produce than a watermelon slipped out of someone's hands, smashing all over the floor.

"It's okay," Agatha said amiably. "Just take another. It's fine. It happens all the time." The young man looked embarrassed and his face was red. "Are you sure?"

"Yes."

Agatha used a dust pan and a mop and slopped the mess into a tomato box. She used tomato boxes all the time because they were good and strong and mostly waterproof and they had cutouts for the hands so they were easy to carry too. She felt good about giving the watermelon to the young man. It was store policy but it made the whole day seem more rewarding, instilling in her a sense of satisfaction. She'd easily turned a small disaster into a giving, pleasant experience.

On her walk home, she clutched her little brown purse in the same desperate way, hardly realizing it was colder. Darkness was pressing, but there was enough blue in the sky to suggest day wasn't quite over. A swath of gold seemed to cling to the horizon as if holding on for dear life. She was thinking about going to bingo. She still had some money, enough at least for that. Maybe she'd be lucky. The thought was exciting and her pace quickened. Now, there was nothing else, just herself and this titillating plan about going out tonight.

When she entered the apartment, she was greeted by the lingering smells of cooking. She was tremendously aware of the warmth and glad to be home. She took off her shoes and set them on the rubber mat with the others. She arranged them all neatly. Then she slipped out of her coat and hung it in the closet amid the clinking of bare hangers. Grant wasn't home, she could tell, nor was Tamara.

She found a scribbled note stuck on the refrigerator. Tamara would be eating at her boyfriend's. That was not a surprise, it happened so often. And Grant, she knew, just wasn't home yet from work. Perhaps if she got supper ready without more ado, she could make it out before he got back. He'd definitely try and talk her out of going and she didn't feel like she should have to spar with him to earn her way.

There were hotdogs and buns in the freezer. She'd thaw them in the microwave and make a salad too. Grant would appreciate that. She ate in a while herself, anxious about the time. She kept glancing at the clock in the microwave, hoping, hoping. She'd put too much dressing on her salad and it was tart on her tongue. After, she left everything there on the table, dirty dish and all, and a note too. And then she slipped back into her shoes and coat and, clutching her purse, left the apartment.

The bus was running late and she waited in a glass shelter with two other women and a man, and a couple teenagers who were smoking. It was cold and she couldn't stop shivering. She hated the smell of the cigarettes too, the smoke lingering in the air in acrid clouds. They weren't supposed to smoke in these things but she wasn't going to say anything. Definitely not. The young man had a blotchy tattoo on his neck, like a dark stain, and his girlfriend purple hair. They were young, she reasoned, things like that were important.

She was shocked not to have the right change, short twenty-five cents, and could have sworn there'd been two quarters in her purse. The bus driver, a plump middle-aged woman with nondescript brown hair, said it was fine, she could come good next time. Amazingly, the young man with the ugly tattoo came forward and with a smile slipped a quarter into the slot for her.

"Thank-you!" she said with a stunned look. "I appreciate it!"

"You're welcome," he smiled, and went back to sit with his girlfriend.

As the bus clunked along in the darkness, she found herself mulling over the good turn. She was sitting just behind the couple. Maybe they're married, she thought. Though they seemed kind of young. She couldn't get a look at their hands to see if there were rings. She wished them the best. They looked nonconformist and he was very nice. Maybe they knew her daughter. She wasn't going to ask.

They got off short of a busy comer. She peered out the window and watched them. They walked away hand in hand. She couldn't remember the last time she and Grant had gone for a walk and held hands.

After a couple of games in the big bright bingo hall, home of a defunct supermarket, she had the feeling it was not going to be her night. She'd missed a couple of straight liners by a single number. She chided herself for coming and not paying attention to the ace of hearts. Glancing at it, she saw that it was still turned face down. She tried flipping it over but it seemed stuck. She let it go.

The place was bright and relatively full of people. She noticed that most of the players were women. It was always that way. And scattered among them were a few men. Bingo didn't seem to be their game. That, at least, was her observation. She wondered how many of the women there were like herself, in tough marriages and always short of money. Probably most. It was consoling and it was sad.

The games wore on, the caller's voice monotone, like a recording, starkly indifferent to the plights of the players. She could feel the aloofness. It was a business of course, there was no time for any empathy. By the end of the evening she'd won nothing and rode the bus home more or less empty-handed.

Grant was a diesel mechanic and worked for a trucking company on the edge of the city, not far from the encroaching new subdivisions. He'd talk about the houses now and again in a spiteful, almost amazed way. The thrust of what he had to say stemmed from funding. "Where in the hell are they gettin' all the money?"

His dirty boots were on the mat. She could smell oil. She took off her shoes and arranged the footwear. Tamara was not home yet. Not to worry as it wasn't very late. She slipped out of her coat, hung it up, then moved tentatively into the apartment. He'd left the dishes. They were still on the table, as were the ketchup, mustard, and relish. Several diced bits of onion lingered on a small dish. She could hear the TV from the bedroom.

When she saw him lying on the bed, she realized how susceptible she was to his looks. He was ruggedly handsome, with a square chin and high cheekbones, short black hair and longish sideburns, and a moustache that tumbled down either side of his mouth turning into a neat, close-cropped goatee. His dark eyes were soft and shy. He had changed into jeans and a T-shirt. She could smell beer.

"How did work go?" she asked, taking up position at the foot of the bed.

"The same," he said. "A helluva lot to do….How much did you win?"

She blushed and could feel it. “I didn’t win a thing. I went to bingo. It’s not as bad as the casino and it lasts longer. Did Tamara call?”

“No,” he said.

She sensed he was okay. He wasn’t drunk and didn’t seem to mind talking. The TV behind her babbled on. It was the twenty-four hour news channel. She shut it out of her mind.

“Did you work late, Grant?”

“Nah. A half-hour maybe. I went for a couple of beers.”

“By yourself?”

“With a couple o’ the guys.”

“The store was busy enough,” she told him. “I don’t make much and it’s a lot of work.”

“There’s not enough for you to stay home. If you ever want a house, I mean….”

“I haven’t entirely forgotten about it,” she said. “It’s become a dream. I don’t want to give up on it though.”

“You never know,” he said, wagging his head smugly.

She could see that he was trying to listen to the TV. He was squinting and his eyes were not on

her.

“I’m going to go and clean up,” she said.

Later on they made love in the dark. The TV was off and it was quiet, except for brief gusts of wind that sighed around the eaves. She heard Tamara come in.

Chapter Two

Tamara lay in bed, afraid. Her TV with its bright, clear picture and chattering people was small consolation. Tears stood in the corners of her eyes, inflating like tiny balloons, ready almost to dribble down her cheeks. She was trembling. She'd known since morning. It had been all she could do then to act normally. The thought that she might make a good actress brought a wry smile to her face. Ethan promised he was going to stand by her and she had every reason to believe him. He'd not lied to her yet about anything or deceived her, nor had he ever been late for a date. He was shocked when she'd told him.

"Are you sure? Can't those things be wrong?"

"I don't think so," she'd cried on his shoulder.

He'd held her tightly as they stood in the dark porch at the back of the house where, in the summertime, his little cousin had dropped a whole gallon of milk on his way out to the party in the yard. The plastic jug had burst open like a bomb and the milk had puddled on the planks. The boy had jumped back, shrieking, then stood there perfectly still, looking terrified, his arms stiff at his sides, fists clenched, as if some other more awful thing might come next.

She caressed her flat stomach, finding it hard to believe that there was something in there, something that was going to grow.

Not only was she afraid, she felt helpless, as if invaded by an enemy and unable to fight back. Removal had only been a fleeting thought, suppressed at once. There was just so much to think about. She could not deal with it all tonight, alone here as she was in the dark room.

She tried to sleep but it would not come. She kept thinking about Ethan. She'd ruined his life. He'd wanted to become a lawyer, like his father. His father had spurred him on in his choice of career. Now, what would happen? How would it all come about? There was no answer.

He called her early in the morning. She was startled out of a sound sleep by her mother. "Tamara, wake up. Ethan is on the phone."

She felt someone nudging her shoulder and slowly opened her eyes. "I'm so tired," she sputtered.

"Ethan is on the phone. He says it's important. Do you want me to tell him you'll call him back?"

She came to her senses, reality returning with a blow. She propped herself up. Her eyes hurt from crying. "I'll come and get the phone," she said.

As soon as her mother left, she got out of bed. She put her hand on her stomach, suddenly aware of what was going on. She was shaky and slightly nauseous. She padded out of the bedroom and slipped into the next room, flipping on the light and easing the door closed.

The room was used mostly for storage. It was small and cluttered, like a box into which you could not put much more. On the single bed there was a heap of boxes crammed full of books and magazines, and big garbage bags bulging with old clothes. There was a plastic laundry hamper too, overflowing with shoes. Amazingly, there was still room for the computer, squeezed up against the wall on a wobbly table. Picking up the phone, Tamara ignored the acorn beside the monitor, another of her mother's good luck charms.

"Hi," she said. "*....Got it, mom!*"

She heard a clunk, then, "I love you."

"I'm so afraid, Ethan, so afraid." She kept her voice down, almost to a whisper. "I hardly slept. All I could think of was you. It was terrible, so terrible....What's going to happen to us?"

"We'll talk about it later," he said, trying his best to soothe.

She wanted to converse but held her tongue. "You're right, this isn't the time."

"I just wanted to tell you that."

"I love you too."

After, she went back and sat on the edge of her bed. She wanted to cry but could not. She was sad and her fear had subsided to manageable anxiety. Though nothing had changed, things did not seem as bad. She noticed thin lines of dawn squeezing through the blinds. It was a new day. The dark of night and all it had portended was draining away. She managed to dredge up, like sunken treasure, what little hope remained.

She had breakfast with her mother at the battered table in the kitchen. She found she had not lost her appetite at all. She had two pieces of toast swathed thickly with peanut butter and a cup of coffee whitened with milk. Her mother wanted to talk but *she* did not. She wasn't nasty, only contributing to the conversation in bits and dribbles. Her mind was on other things, not on what, now, seemed to be trivialities.

"Dad's already at work," her mother told her.

"Mmm hmm." Looking at her mom sitting there with sleepy eyes and blond, dishevelled hair, she wondered if she had ever lived with a big secret. If she had ever put on a good act to get through a day.

"You've got plenty of time, Tamara. By the way, what did Ethan want so early?"

"Nothing really," she said.

She worked slowly on the last piece of toast, savoring the peanut butter. It was delicious. It was amazing how something so plain and simple could be so uplifting. Her mother probably thought something was up. Like she and Ethan had had a spat. Hardly imagining the truth. She shuddered momentarily.

"Have you noticed the Christmas decorations?"

"Yup."

"So darn early! Too early, don't you think?"

"I guess."

"You're not very talkative."

She shrugged. "Nothing to say."

"Why don't I believe you?"

She sipped the coffee, her dark eyes lowered to the table, her long black hair falling forward like a silky veil.

"What would you like for Christmas, Tamara?"

She pouted, glanced up at her mother for a second and said, "A new top or something maybe."

"I saw some the other day at the mall. In that shop you like. I'll check them out. They looked

real cool."

"That'd be nice."

"More coffee?"

"Okay."

There was silence. All they could hear were a neighbor's garbled words and a baby wailing down the hail. Tamara had a start. Cripes, she thought, I can hardly stand it!

"Homework all done?"

"Only had a little."

"Did you do it at Ethan's"

"Yes," she said, forcing a smile.

Her mother checked the clock. "Well, it's getting on."

"I'm ready."

"Dress warm. It's gotten colder."

"Sure."

She left for the bus on time. She wore her uniform—gray slacks, a white blouse with a navy sweater overtop—and a black pea jacket.

"Bye, dear," her mom said, smacking a little kiss on her cheek and holding her arm.

"Good-bye."

Clutching her binder, Tamara descended the steps more slowly than usual. She definitely did not want to fall. She wondered if subconsciously she was preparing to become a mother. The idea seemed ludicrous but she could not laugh. It was a stark, new reality.

She stepped quickly out in the cold, squeezing her arms up against her body and lowering her chin into her jacket. She glanced down at the corner and saw a boy and a girl. They were not standing together. She wished she were them. They most likely did not have a heavy burden. Nothing like her. What they might be considering as worrisome—a project that was due soon or a test—was nothing at all. She couldn't understand it: they'd been using condoms and following the rules. She should have been taking birth control pills. If only she could go back! If only!

The school bus was beginning to fill. She sat at the front with the other girls in a seat by herself. It was cold in the bus and the windows were steamy. The world outside looked like it was in a fog. She tried to keep a happy face. As the bus sped along, rattling and banging even over the slightest bumps, she chatted with everyone. They had their plans, centering mostly around social events. Movies, of course. A dance somewhere.

The coffee shop. It all sounded so good to her, so carefree and innocent. She felt like a black sheep. She could still take part in things; nothing much was off limits. And life would go on. She could choose to be happy or sad—friendly and outgoing or all into herself to the exclusion of everyone and everything else.

Ethan did not take the bus to school. He lived close, in the new subdivision behind it. He was waiting for her at the door, milling about in a group, but he broke away like a grape from a bunch as soon as he saw her.

He kissed her on the cheek. "You're cold!" He put his arm around her and drew her quickly into the bright, warm foyer. "This is better. Are you alright?"

"I'm so afraid, Ethan."

"Don't be. We can do this. We can get through it, Tamara."

He sounded so convincing she had to smile despite it all. It was good to be in the school. She didn't feel quite so all alone or afraid. Everyone seemed a friend. There were conversations and chortles of laughter. It seemed that none of what had happened could be true. She could kid herself and pretend and perhaps even come close for a moment to completely believing.

"What's your first class?" he asked.

"Religion," she said, wagging her head. "So ironic I can hardly stand it."

Ethan was not smiling. He looked analytical. His brows were slightly stitched and his mouth was closed. She knew he would take this hard. He took off his rectangular glasses and held them up to the light, squinted at them with his pensive brown eyes, then put them back on.

"You're going to have to get some confirmation," he told her.

"I'll call today."

"I can come with you."

"Of course," she said. "I'm not going to be able to do this alone."

"You won't have to."

He took her hand and they walked across the bright polished floor to the hallway and the lockers.

Ethan couldn't concentrate. He was sitting up straight, his hands folded on the desk, and his eyes fixed on the pretty, young, first-year teacher. She was giving a spiel on the history of communism. Ordinarily he would have been interested in anything that had to do with politics, as politics and law went hand in hand. But today his mind was on the 'mess' he was in. He hated to think of it that way. He loved Tamara, there wasn't any question. Perhaps he ought to think of it as an entanglement that just had to be disentangled. At first, the spinoff of consequences had not dawned on him. But the more he pondered, the worse it seemed. How had it happened in the first place? Now *that* angered him. He'd been careful. The condoms had always been on properly, none had slipped off, nor had any broken either. He squeezed his hands together until they ached. He was a Catholic. She was a Catholic. Abortion was an economic solution. It had already invaded his mind. He was certain, however, that no one would go for it, except perhaps—and it was a big 'perhaps'—himself. Tamara might initially. In the end she would not.

There'd be little in the way of a social life. His parents would support him emotionally and financially, but he had awful visions of himself stuck in a small apartment somewhere with a squawling baby, changing shitty diapers while his wife, which she would become, made supper. *That* she could do! He smiled at the thought that she actually was a very good cook. It was, however, not the kind of life he'd had in mind for himself. It was astonishing how fast everything had changed. His dreams had shattered like a crystal vase. There would be few outings anymore with friends. And money would be spent on *important* things. 'Rent' was a word that loomed up before him like an approaching storm. And the word 'groceries' was hardly appealing. There would be no BMW or Mini Cooper. And becoming a lawyer seemed next to impossible. Loans would have to be sought out. And there would be no freewheeling. It would be straight to school and straight home. And how on earth would Tamara get *her* education?

He was depressed. He loved her. But he just didn't know. Perhaps he was putting the cart before the horse. He told himself to take things one day at a time, not to look ahead. It wasn't easy. He glanced around the classroom. Everyone else seemed now to have an advantage over him. As in a horse race, they were several lengths ahead. That was how he saw it. He knew he would have to reach deep down inside himself and gather up all his strength and force of will for the biggest challenge yet.

Grant had taken the day off. It was already November and he still had three vacation days for the year. After a breakfast of eggs, toast, and coffee, he left everything on the table and went into the bedroom to get his gun. The bed was unmade and for all he cared it could stay that way. Agatha could make it when she got home. He opened the closet doors, lifted a couple of clumps of clothing off the top shelf, dropped them on the floor, and pulled out the rifle case.He carried it back to the kitchen, unzipped it, and took the rifle out. The rifle was good and solid, the right weight, a real killing machine. He gloated over it for a moment, his eyes widening like a child holding a new toy. A somewhat sinister smile played on his mouth. He sat down and took aim at the window, putting his fmger on the trigger. Squinting, one eye closed, he could see the window lock in the crosshairs of the scope. He couldn't wait to fire it again. He felt a rush of adrenaline. It would be soon enough.The rifle was a Remington Model 700 SPS Stainless, the 'SPS' standing for Special Purpose Synthetic. It was resting across his knees. He loved its sleek, silvery, almost futuristic look. The barrel was made of stainless steel, bright and clean, the stock gray and synthetic. He marvelled that something so beautiful, so peaceful and innocent-looking, could be so deadly. He decided to clean out the muzzle with a brush and some black powder soap.

When he was done he left the rifle on the counter, went to the spare bedroom, and brought back a tiny can of machine oil. He took extra good care of his rifle. It was important to him and brought him enjoyment. The rifle had only been fired a few times and he knew he could have let the cleaning go, but he wouldn't have felt right. He had a compulsion and went about finishing the job, squeezing out a drop of oil here and another there and then wiping down the barrel with a paper towel. He liked the sweet smell of the oil. He brought the towel up to his nose and sniffed it. It called to mind machines that were cared for and worked well, their interconnected parts moving in conjunction with one another smoothly and almost inaudibly. He imagined how the parts of the rifle worked together in an efficient, noiseless way to bring about death. It was like magic. And he was infatuated.

He put the rifle and the paraphernalia away and went into the living-room to play a video game. It was one in which you had to shoot and kill first or be killed. He'd played it so often he was an expert. He seldom played badly and when he did he got angry. He would call himself a "stupid son of a bitch" or a "bearing head". He sat down on the floor with the control in his hands. He could feel his heart beating faster. The TV monitor was an escape from reality and took him to a building of dusky corridors that intersected one another and rooms with open doorways from which enemies might pop out. There were zigzagging stairways and gaping elevator doors. Even parked vehicles where killers lurked in the shadows.

The shooting soon began in earnest. He loved the loud reports of guns going off, watching empty shells popping out and clanking onto the floor, and hearing the curt click-clack of reloading. The phone rang. He ignored it. He shot a man in the chest and he crumbled to the floor, lifeless as a rag doll, his sub machine gun clanging on a railing and falling somewhere through darkness. There was a bright red circle where the bullet had entered and blood was splattered everywhere. Stepping past the body to the next ambush, Grant took a cautious peek inside an elevator. Nothing. He trudged on, his automatic pistol at the ready. A door groaned open. He stopped, waited, inched up, finger on the trigger, ducked in to shoot, but there was no one. And then he heard the shot and knew the groaning door had been a ploy to distract him. He had lost the game. He was dead.

"Fuck!" he yelled, and threw the control onto the sofa.

He met his friend at the bar a few minutes after noon. Silas was an autoworker and had also taken the day off. He never called him Silas. He went by Slim. That was what he liked. He was tall and thin and Grant thought the nickname was perfect. Even Slim thought so. Three of the letters from his real name, he liked to say, were also in his nickname. "Just call me Slim, b'Jesus. Just call me Slim."

They sat at the bar on the hard wooden stools and had their draft beer in tall glasses. The place was quiet, just waking up it seemed to Grant. There was still lots of hope and promise in the day. He watched the two older men across from them struggling with sandwiches. The one with the bushy white eyebrows over sunken eyes was a miserable sucker, he could just tell. His friend (if he was) was much better-dressed and nodded with a smile as the waitress cruised by inquiring as to how they were doing. Mr. Bushy Eyebrows' face, however, was set in a stony scowl, and he never so much as glanced at Clo. Grant chuckled.

"I bet that old bugger there with the snowy eyebrows is a miserable son of a bitch."

"Ya think?"

"Take a look."

Slim, with his fidgety little eyes, squinted at the man. "B'Jesus, you're probably right. You got a talent for that kind o' thing, Grant. Tellin' what a person's like by lookin' at their face and knowin' what's goin' on in their head too. He don't look too kind, do he? Gummin' that sandwich. Got bad teeth too, b'Jesus. Huh!"

The River Memory was old and seedy and everything in it either needed refurbishing or replacement. Grant liked it nonetheless. It was a kind of home away from home where everyone knew everyone else and most of their business too. It was comforting to know he could go there and talk about things to just about anyone. And the waitress, the one working now, was not hard to look at. Clo, short for Clotilda, was the wife of the owner, who was doing the bartending. He'd heard she did a little 'playing around' from people whose stories he was inclined to believe.

"What're we eatin', Grant?"

Clo was standing in front of the cantankerous looking oldtimer.

"He's gonna spout off at her, Slim, I can tell," Grant said. "Just wait and see."

The man erupted like a volcano: "It's too hard! Overcooked! Burnt! Look!" He flung aside the top of the sandwich and poked the bacon with his finger. "Black, see? Black!"

Clo told him apologetically she'd go and get him another one.

He shook his head disgustedly. "Ah, to hell with it!"

Clo turned away with an amused smile on her rosy round cheeks. Grant winked at her. He knew she was used to dealing with obnoxious customers. He liked flirting with her. He could tell she was interested. She had big round breasts and always wore shirts and blouses that showed them off. The rest of her wasn't bad either. Though plump, she was proportionate. From time to time he got the feeling she was ready and then she would kind of shy away. As if the edge of the precipice was too close. He figured that sooner or later he would get her into the sack.

"You were right, b'Jesus," Slim said. "You predicted what he was gonna do." Out of the blue, he called over to Clo and ordered twenty chicken wings and a pizza with everything on it except pineapple. He tapped his glass. "A couple more o' these too."

"How do you know I want chicken wings, Slim?"

"Hey, remember that night you went in that store tuh get smokes 'n that kid was standin' out front and you come out 'n said he was up to no good?"

"I sure do."

"That there store was robbed that night, b'Jesus! And what about blond Freddy? Remember him, Grant?"

Grant had to remind himself that that was what beer did to Slim. He became even more hyperactive. "How could anyone forget Freddy, Slim?"

"You said he seemed real depressed, you did, b'Jesus."

"Yup."

"And sure as winter comes he went out 'n killed himself. Kind o' like you predicted he would. You got a gift there, Grant."

"Probably just good guessing."

They ate their lunch and drank their beer, and soon there was a plateful of tiny, gnawed bones on the bar along with a few pizza crusts. Slim could not eat crust because his teeth were poor. Meantime, more people had filtered in. Some for lunch and some to stay and drink. And another waitress was on the scene to help out. Her name was Eileen and she had short, white, bleached-out blond hair pulled back and squeezed into a little nub. She liked to drink and her face, thought Grant, showed it. It was pale and gaunt and her eyes were like two sunken holes in her head. She looked like death warmed over. She lived alone and he felt kind of sorry for her.

"Noisier now, Slim."

"Let's go out for a smoke."

Slim did not wait. He got right up and hurried down the short corridor and out the back door. In due time, Grant followed.

They had their cigarettes in the cold without jackets on. Slim said he was going to quit. Grant paid no attention. He knew his pal wouldn't have said a thing if it weren't so cold. Grant liked to smoke. He drew long and hard on the filter and inhaled deeply, letting the smoke out in billows that rose like tiny clouds and disappeared somewhere up against the cloudy sky. There was a parking lot at the back, A few people trickled in and out and Grant acknowledged them with a kind nod. He knew some by name, others by appearance. Slim seemed indifferent. He turned, pretending he didn't see them. He couldn't stand still. He kept shifting his weight from foot to foot in a little spot dance, eager for something. Grant watched as he flicked his head one way and then another, looking mostly at the sky as if trying to spot something erratic.

"I cleaned my gun today," Grant told him, rubbing the butt of his cigarette into the heaved patio stone with his foot, "and it's ready to go. Next week one day, I hope."

"Gotta get the permit."

"It's coming."

"Hey, Grant, yuh hear the shots in the mornin'?"

"Sometimes, yeah."

"B'Jesus, it Bet's me goinl…Let's git inside."

Slim bounced away and Grant followed right after, musing about what a nut his friend was. He chuckled. He liked him enough. There was even a bit of Slim in himself.

Chapter Three

The doctor was in his forties, a good-looking man in navy blue chinos and a white shirt. He wore wire rim glasses and his hair was dark and longish, combed back, with a sophisticated touch of silver at the temples. Perhaps it was the silver that gave Tamara the impression he was old as he told her from his desk she was definitely pregnant. His words made it official, but she was not shocked. Embarrassed, rather. He was a grown-up man, a father figure, and he *knew.* She could feel her face turning red. She wanted to crawl under the desk and hide. Hide from the world.

"You're healthy," he said, "and you should have no problem. I'm fully aware of your situation. Everything will work out, we'll see to it. You can come to me anytime."

It all sounded simple enough. But she was the one who would have to deal with her parents—and Ethan's. They'd all thought so highly of her too! She felt terrible.

Ethan was in the waiting room, a chair away from an older woman who was perusing a magazine. She could see he was anxious. He was sitting up straight as a statue, his hands clasped in his lap, and his leg bobbing up and down. He got right to his feet.

"Yes," she whispered, moving on by him and out the door.

In the hallway he clasped her arm and she turned around.

There was a look of helplessness on her ashen face. "What now?" she demanded, frowning up into his troubled eyes.

"We'll get through it," he told her. "We'll do everything right. It will be one step at a time. One, two, three. Like that. We will have to tell them. You will have to tell yours first. And then I'll tell mine. We can do it, Tamara . Yes we can."

She believed him. He sounded so sure of himself. And was so handsome, how could anyone resist the charm? It was at moments like this that she realized how lucky she was to have him. He hadn't run off. Nor had he suddenly avoided her, refusing to communicate. That had been one of her

greatest fears. She would have been alone and that would have made all of this so much more frightening. With the shadow of a beard, he looked especially kind and sweet. She put her arms around him and kissed him full on the lips.

"I believe you," she said. "You always sound so sure of everything."

After supper that evening she went to her room to study for a test. The wind had picked up and the screen in the window chattered. She was sitting on her bed in jeans and a T-shirt and with black and white striped stockings on her feet. Her jeans felt snug, and she wondered if her mind was playing tricks on her. It couldn't possibly be because of the pregnancy. She put her notebook down and sat there with her arms folded. It made her think. She felt panicky. She wouldn't be able to dress the same. Her life was going to be a lot different. She hated upset stomachs. Perhaps she would be spared the affliction. She glanced around the room. Everything in it was representative of the different eras in her life. A doll she'd played with as a child sat in a little red plastic chair, dressed in a blue and white checked dress with ruffled sleeves. Her grade eight graduation photo smiled out from the wall. It had been fun then. She'd liked a boy named Robert. Tears welled up in her eyes and she wiped them away with a finger. The other photos brought back memories too: her cat Cannel who'd died of leukemia a couple of years back, a holiday in Florida, her grandparents who lived in Barrie, and her grandmother in Fort Erie. She scanned the books on top of her desk, in a neat row like quiet children. Some she'd read way back in elementary school, others more recently. There was one era after another. Her artwork —drawings in pencil, crayon, charcoal, and pastel; and oil paintings in cheap frames—leaned up against a wall like troubling images of a former, secure life. She didn't have to look in her drawers to know that in them lingered clothing all washed and neatly folded that she would never wear again—things she'd outgrown or that were worn out. She kept them because they'd been favorites. And now they were colorful mementos. An old plastic watch she'd gotten early in the primary grades lay curled in a clear plastic case in front of the books. It would probably work. All it needed was some light repair. It likely wouldn't fit however nor would it look right either. She was sixteen after all. She was no longer the wide-eyed innocent little girl she'd been a short time ago. Oh, *how* she wished she *were* though! She wouldn't be sitting here in a dither, breathing so uneasily. Her first boyfriend had given her the ring with the pearl. She still wore it. As she gazed at it, it seemed so innocent, a tiny white eye in a circle of gold, unencumbered, open to the world. It had no secrets, nothing to hide. She pored over her stuffed animals to momentarily free her mind. They brought her a smile. She secured her long black hair behind her ears and tilted her head reflectively. They were all puppies with colorful, pretty ribbons round their necks, propped up along her footboard like a small watchful family. Her large teddy bear, Alex, towered over all of them. He would be forever a symbol of the time she'd had her tonsils taken out. He was the one she'd talked to at night when she was all alone in the hospital. She could touch him, even now, and she knew it would help.

Tamara took up her notebook again. She had to study, she knew that. She had to concentrate. Marks were important to her. She still wanted to be something; what, she didn't know. A career of some kind. With what had come up, she had to try more to live in the moment. She could not let herself be consumed by what she saw as a setback. She'd heard the expression "some good comes out of everything". She just had to believe that. She told herself she would get through it all and things would be okay.

She had lunch with her dad on Saturday. She'd made French toast, which he loved, and fried some sweet mini breakfast sausages to go with it. The kitchen smelled like maple syrup.

"Yummy," he said as he sat down at the table. "I don't get this very often. Usually it's a cold egg salad sandwich or ham and cheese. This is a helluva treat, let me tell you!" He noticed she wasn't eating. "What's the matter, Tamara? You're not gonna let me eat alone, are you?"

"Well," she said, wagging her head, "I had a cup of coffee a little while ago and half of an orange."

"How long d'you think that'll keep you goin'?"

"Maybe in a while I'll have something else."

Grant poured plenty of imitation maple syrup on his French toast and pretty soon his plate looked like a shallow amber pond. His hair, because it was short, didn't look messy. Still it was easy for Tamara to tell that he'd just gotten out of bed. His eyes squinted in the light and there were dark crescents under them too. He needed a shave, definitely. His T-shirt was wrinkled, as if he'd slept in it, and he had on the baggy old sweat pants he shuffled around the house in.

She watched him eat. He cut things up in large hunks and chewed in a hurry, the coin-sized muscles on the sides of his face throbbing like a baby's heart. A wave of fear shot through her. How could she tell them? She couldn't imagine gathering enough courage. Her palms felt clammy as did her face. She was breathing faster too. It bothered her to think she was keeping a secret. She would've rather they knew. Here she was with a baby inside her and her dad was right there across the table. It seemed like the ultimate in deceit.

"I am going hunting next week," he told her, looking up.

"I hate when you go hunting, daddy," she said. It was another cause for anxiety. "I'm always so afraid you're going to get hurt. I can hardly stand it. Well..."

"Friday," he said. "Silas and me. Over to the island. We'll have meat to eat this winter." He smiled broadly. She wondered if her baby would look like him. "There's only so many permits and only so many hunters allowed out there at one time. It cuts the risk down for shooting accidents."

"Don't even mention it," she said, getting up. "Would you like your coffee?"

"Okay," he said.

By the time he was done sopping up the last of the syrup with the remaining couple of wedges

of French toast, the coffee was in front of him in a husky white mug, the one he liked. "I can't understand you not eating," he said. "It was damn

good, lemme tell you!"

"I'm so glad you liked it," she said. "I still wish you wouldn't go."

"Hunting? Of course I'm going. Only a bearing head wouldn't go. It's a golden opportunity. D'you know, Tamara, that some people travel thousands of miles every fall to go deer hunting and here I have it just a couple miles away?"

"It doesn't make it any safer though."

There was a pause and her dad sat back, rubbing his black little chin beard. The silence bothered her because she could see he was using it to think and assess. From time to time he'd glance over at her with those penetrating eyes of his and she'd look away, over at the sink or window, or down at the floor, bending once to pick up an imaginary crumb. Her dad made her feel uncomfortable with those eyes of his. She felt like he was seeing right into her soul.

"What're you going to do today?" he asked finally, his cup up by his hairy chin. She was glad he'd broken the frigid silence.

"Pm going to the movies with Ethan,"' she said. "Not until after supper though. I've got some homework to do at the computer and my room's a mess."

"I bet!" he laughed. "When is *your* room ever a mess?"

"It *is,* dad!" and she had to laugh too.

"I doubt it, Tamara. I doubt it to hell and back."

"Got a poppy?"

"I forgot. I ought to have one too. I was gonna buy one yesterday, dammit all!" "You can have mine."

"No, I'll get one. It's Remembrance Day and I've been seem' them everywhere all week. Like little red eyes. Hell, hell, hell!"

"It's not the end of the world."

"It's called respect and I ought to've been thinkin' about others, not just myself."

After the dishes were all done and put away where they belonged, Tamara went to her room. She made her bed and tidied up and brought her dirty clothes to the hamper in the spare bedroom. It was the wannest room in the apartment. But she *so* wanted to clear it up. It had gotten to the point where she shuddered at the thought of going into it. She shook her head, looking at the computer. She hated using it in here. She wondered why her mom kept all the junk. If only she'd get rid of the bags of clothes! Just *that* would make a big difference.

She went back to her room and stood there gazing at a picture of Ethan that she had on her dresser. It was a casual photo in a silver frame. He was in jeans and a T-shirt, standing down at the river's edge beside a large boulder on which his hand rested. He was going to be a father and she found that hard to believe. He seemed so young. He *was* so young. Of course he was! What was she thinking? And so was she.

She sat on the bed still looking at him. Her dad would understand, she was pretty sure. At the right moment anyhow. He was upset that he didn't have a poppy for Remembrance Day. To remember the dead soldiers. Now *that* was altruistic sure enough. He wouldn't condemn her. He would help her. Her mom was the same. She didn't really have to worry about her either. There might be a rattle of disapproval out of her, firm words, but no loud roar or anything like that. She wished her dad would stop his drinking. Though he'd been a little better lately. There'd been no loud arguments between him and her mom, no slamming of doors on his part or smacking walls with his hand. It made her shudder to think of how he could get when he drank too much.

Agatha had had a busy day and by four, with just an hour to go, she was more than ready to leave. Saturday was always like that. The consolation was that the time went fast. She'd practically never stopped. She was on her way over to the walk-in cooler when she met Nathan. He was standing there talking to an older woman by a chest cooler that was stocked with hot dogs and cold lunch meat. He held out his hand to stop her while he went on chatting.

"....I'm sorry about it. It wasn't selling and I know we're not gonna get any more."

The woman smiled and said, "Well, I guess I can do without. Thank you, Nathan," and hobbled away up the aisle.

"What time you done, Aggy?" he wanted to know.

She was taken aback. She'd not expected it. "I finish at five," she told him, avoiding his eyes and looking off to the side at nothing in particular.

"Let's go out somewhere."

That was it. That was the invitation she'd been kind of waiting for for a while. The one she'd been thinking of tendering too. "Where?"

"For a ride," he said "Can you?"

She said "Yes" without considering. There was no room for a pause or to delay. "I'll call home and tell them. Not a problem at all."

"Great!...A secret, okay?"

"Of course."

He picked her up a couple of blocks away, at a church cemetery where even the white old cracked and broken tombstones looked nearly black in the dusk of the quickly fading November day. He drove a small Ford two-door, and when she saw it roll up alongside the curb, she came out like a robber from behind the trunk of a large oak tree. She glanced around to be sure there was no one about and quickly padded across the hard frozen ground to the car.

He drove down the street, not saying much, the radio turned low, and then he went over the bridge that spanned Awappich creek and along the road to a park by the water. She was a bit afraid, she had to admit, but not of him. Her fear was coming more from the thought of someone seeing them. But she managed to talk herself out of the silliness when he pulled up and parked a way from the road and she saw that they were alone with the darkness falling all around them. She took a deep breath and could feel herself beginning to unwind. He left the motor running for heat and shut the lights off.

She was surprised when he kissed her. It happened that she was turning her head toward him at the same time as he was turning his and the kiss landed smack on her lips. He seemed hungry for her but she drew away. The kiss had excited her and intimidated her too. She felt like giving in he was *so* good looking! But she was not promiscuous. And she knew if she let him have his way it might end right there.

"What's up, Aggy? Why're we here?"

"Let's just talk for now, okay?" she told him. "I hope you're not offended."

"No way."

They chatted about everything, daily things like work, life at home, his mother and father, her husband, her daughter—her marriage in general—and the fact he was presently not seeing anyone. "My only question is why not, Nathan?"

"I best let you know I'm picky about women," he told her. "I like 'em older and most of them that I've met are married—just like you. The younger ones, the good lookin' ones that is, they're all taken too. And the ones that aren't are either not too good lookin' or silly or a little of both."

"Silly?" she chuckled. "The right one just hasn't come around yet. She will."

There was silence. In the darkness of the car she could see his head was turned to her. She wanted to tell him that if he was looking for a longterm relationship, a serious one, then dating someone married was not a good idea. The woman would most likely not leave her husband if there was a lot to lose—family, say, or money. Or would go back to him eventually. She knew, however, there were exceptions.

"Are you the right one, Aggy?"

"I'm already married," she said on a more serious note. "I can't leave. In a way I love him. He just has these mad jags when he's been drinking. It's not cool to be there when it happens. It would sure be nice if he gave it up....I'm looking for an escape, which is how I feel about it. But I don't want to give it all up. I don't want to throw away what I have. He can be cool too. And there's Tamara. I have to think about her. She'd be destroyed if I ever left Grant."

"You're not happy or you wouldn't be here, Aggy."

"I just want something light. A little fun," she added. "nothing too heavy. But I don't just want it once. I want there to be a book full of

pages, not just a note on a page to toss away."

"Hey, I understand," he said, and kissed her. "I'm gonna be the one to write the book." "Is this the first chapter?'

"You betcha!"

Chapter Four

There was a big fight that night. It was late, after midnight, and Tamara wasn't home. Agatha was glad she wasn't around because it kind of took the edge off things. All the time it was going on—the yelling, the name calling, the accusations—she fretted over the possibility her daughter might walk in. Grant had flipped the light on and was standing at the foot of the bed stabbing his finger at her like a dictator, his body convulsing wildly as if he was possessed. He was just livid with rage and his face was as red as a tomato. She was lying in bed, her eyes squinting in the sudden flood of light.

"You bitch!" he said. "Where in the hell were ya?"

"At the casino," she said, trying to hide her fright.

"I don't believe ya. I called here and there was no goddam answer! Hell, hell, hell! Can't you stay home? Can't you stay home for once?...Okay, okay, okay. How much you win?"

"I lost fourteen dollars."

"Huh! Well I don't goddam believe ya! Ya never lose just fourteen dollars. How long were ya there, Aggy? How long?"

"A couple of hours."

"Then ya probably lost twice that—at *least....Ifyou were there even....Hell,* hell, hell! D'you think I'm a bearing head? Ya wanna get a goddam house, dammit all, and you're out blowin' money! Lemme tell ya, we ain't gonna get no house this way, hell no!"

He punched the mattress and she saw that he was lost for words. He was shaking his head and looking at the floor. And then he stood there like a foreman at a work site poring over things with his arms akimbo. He was scowling at her, waiting for her to speak. She really had nothing to say, knowing it was futile to try and reason with him when he'd had too much to drink. She wanted to avert her eyes but she did not want to give him a victory. She'd learned to control her fear and keep her composure.

"We can talk in the morning, Grant," she managed.

He jabbed his finger at her again and stormed out of the room. A moment later, when she got out of bed to turn out the light, she thought she could hear him gibbering to himself in the living-room above the sound of the TV.

When Tamara came home she knew right away her father'd been on a binge. She said "Hi" to him but he ignored her. He was slouched on the sofa, with his feet up on the coffee table. She went right to her room and shut the door.

In the darkness later on she lay in bed recalling the nice evening she'd had with Ethan. They'd gone and seen a movie at the mall and then to a favorite haunt of theirs for a drink and pizza. She felt guilty now for having had the drink. She wanted to do all the right things and alcohol was not one of them. But Ethan had told her one beer wouldn't matter. Though the evening had gone well she somehow didn't feel it was the same. A dark cloud seemed to hover over her and she could tell that Ethan was preoccupied. He seemed quieter, less given to conversation. Life had suddenly become serious.They'd made love at his house, while his parents slept upstairs. It was always good and she loved sex, though she'd hesitated tonight for fear that it might be harmful to the baby. But Ethan had told her it was all an old wives' tale.

With just bits of street light stealing in through the blinds, it seemed that all there was in the whole world was Ethan, herself, and the baby growing inside her. She was so comfortable and cozy that she forgot for a moment where she was and the trouble in her home. She was glad it had nothing to do with her. They would have to, she and Ethan, adjust to *their* new situation; it was between the two of them, hidden away, a secret. Perhaps that was why it took nine months The adjustment was a long process, she told herself. She was proud of Ethan. He seemed to be okay but she never knew with him. He did a lot of thinking and didn't say very much. Once, they'd been planning to go to a school dance. It was Valentine's, she remembered, and he'd gone right along with the idea, seeming quite enthusiastic, up until the day before. And then he just said he didn't want to go. He'd heard that one of the members of the band was seeing another guy's girlfriend. They'd ended up staying home.

Ethan was having a hard time going to sleep which was unusual after making love. He lay on his back for a while and then rolled onto his side, and finally onto his stomach. He was physically tired enough but his mind was racing along. He belonged to the Drama Club at school and he'd been asked to play the main character in Christmas Comes To Gus McGraw. Of course he'd accepted. He'd read the thing four or five times already to get a feel for the part and that was not counting the other one when the cast had practiced their lines in the classroom. But for him there was so much more to being a good actor. He had to get a grip on what the character was all about. That meant putting himself in their shoes and taking on a whole new personality. And this, so far, he'd been unable to do with

Gus McGraw. He knew it was because of Tamara and the baby, they were just about all he could think about.

A car went quietly by and it seemed as if it had roared right through the bedroom. He loved Tamara and he wanted the baby too. He wondered though how much he was going to have to give up. It scared him thinking about it, just as it did the play. He'd never had such a hard time being 'dramatic' before. He had to admit he really didn't know who this Gus McGraw character was. He could recite lines alright but he couldn't fool anyone. An audience would know if he was 'there' or not. Was it going to be this way for everything now on? Would he have difficulty studying? Performing for the Track Club come spring? And what about that car he'd wanted? To be bought from summer work? Wouldn't that money now have to go somewhere else? He was sad as much as he was apprehensive. Tears came to his eyes and he began to wonder desperately what he'd done. Why was I so foolish? He chided himself and then felt guilty. In his mind he saw Tamara. He owed it to her. He loved her, did he not? And had she not given herself to him completely? He bit down on his lip and told himself he was going to stand by her no matter what.

The new week found Tamara shying away from her dad. His suspicious looks began on Tuesday at supper and carried on more or less throughout the evening anytime she left her room. She knew it couldn't be her shape, it hadn't changed at all. Maybe it was all in her mind, she told herself, the suspicion stuff. However on Friday evening at meal time he came out with it.

"Dammit all, Tamara, you've bin mopin' around here all week! What's goin' on, girl?"

"I haven't been *moping,* dad. Everything is fine....I'm just concerned about the hunting trip."

She felt a sense of relief when he said, “So that’s it! femme tell you, Slim ‘n me are pros.

And…we’re gonna have plenty to eat this winter.”

Chapter Five

Saturday was cold and there was a light fluffy snowfall. Grant left the apartment early in the morning and drove on over to Slim's on the other side of the creek. Slim lived on the upper floor of an old brick duplex that had been painted deep cherry red. The windows were new, with white trim, and the black roof was only a year or so old. All in all, thought Grant, it was a pretty nice place, a bit garish because of the color but in good enough condition. He had it in mind sometimes that he and Agatha could maybe buy a similar house and occupy one of the apartments while the rent from the other pretty much let them live for next to nothing. But as he pulled up in front, he noted how large the lot was and all the grass there would be to cut. He could see autumn leaves too in the thin blanket of new snow, like shavings of chocolate on a cake. He'd seen enough of them squatting around in those bulging paper bags out at the curb on garbage day to know they meant a hell of a lot of work.

It wasn't long before Slim came running out with his rifle case in one hand and his lunch in the other. Grant got out of his rusty old car and opened the trunk for him.

"Throw 'er in there, Slim."

"B'Jesus, it's a cold one! Our goddam fingers're gonna turn tuh icicles."

On the way, it was Slim who did most of the talking.

"Yuh got the permit, huh?"

"It's here."

"B'Jesus, we're lucky! They're darn enough hard tuh get, they are. Gary 'n Len couldn't get 'em. They put their names in too late. What with hearin' about this cull, Grant, they shoulda thought ahead like we did." His hands jittery and grimy with dry worked-in oil, Slim lit a cigarette and the smoke began filling the car. "I hope tuh hell Jason's there. He swore he'd be. Tole me some guys wanna go at six. B'Jesus, it'd still be dark!"

"The wife mind?"

"What?"

"You goin'?"

Slim shook his head vigorously, his dark hair flopping around. "Hell no! She's glad tuh get rid o' me so's she can have some peace. B'Jesus, I'm glad tuh get the hell out o' there too." He laughed insanely and stomped his foot. "Snow's comin' down thicker. They like this. It's their kind o' weather."

They were soon out by the Niagara River. Daylight was beginning to emerge in the form of a dull silvery glow. The snowflakes were zipping up against the windshield like thousands of ineffective little gremlins bent on turning back the expedition.

"Won't be long now, Grant." Slim's little eyes were fixed ahead, trying to burn a beam through the white attack but he could see no further than twenty or thirty feet. "They'll be out in herds, Grant. The trees'll cut the snow. Aiming'11 be easy enough 'n, b'Jesus, we might be able tuh get a step or so closer."

"May be," Grant said, hardly listening.

He was concentrating on the driving. The lines on the road seemed to be jumping right up into his eyes. He was thinking about Tamara. He knew that something was wrong, he wasn't dumb. She'd crossed that fine line revealing just enough of her inner self to let him know. There was the trace of a concern even in her smile. But, about what? He could not figure it out. Perhaps she was upset about himself and Agatha and their little spats. Though they hadn't seemed to bother her in the past. Preoccupation was hiding in the camouflage of a pretty face.

They turned in at the boat launch, which was hardly visible from the road. Jason was not there but there were three pickups parked off to the side and one was his. The boat trailer behind it was empty.

"He's gone across," Slim said with assurance.

Because of the snow they waited inside the car and said nothing at all. Slim was staring ahead, an anxious look on his face, as if there still might be a chance he wouldn't get to go hunting. Grant had no doubt that soon the boat would come puttering over. Meantime, he reasoned that Tamara was still seeing Ethan which meant they hadn't broken up so it couldn't be that. He wondered—and it seemed outrageous because his daughter wasn't that stupid—if she might be pregnant. He tried to dismiss the notion but his mind wouldn't allow for it. He was angry. Tamara was far too young and *that* Ethan there, *he'd* be the one to blame.

Like a lost soul the little boat emerged from the snowy camouflage and came floating up to the dock.

"There's the goddam sailor now!" Slim shouted, and jumped out of the car.

They took their things and went and piled them in the boat. Grant paid Jason and they pushed out into the Niagara river.

The boat puttered along in the snowy dawn, the ink-dark water lapping against it. It was colder than Grant had thought. He sat in the front, with Slim behind, and folded his arms and hugged himself to stave off the chill. He could only think of Tamara. He'd rolled the little snowball of a thought into a colossal boulder of an obsession. That was what it must be. Dammit all, what the hell else? He'd been young once too. They didn't just sit around playing cards. He clenched and unclenched his fists, hardly listening to Jason and Slim prattling. He was ready to throttle Ethan. If only he had his hands on him! It took a few minutes to get to the island and before long Jason was tying off on a post at the shoreline. Grant and Slim grabbed their things and hopped out.

"What time you want me back?" Jason wanted to know.

"Before dark," Grant said. "Around four."

While the boat puttered away, Grant and Slim prepared for the hunt. Grant found that as soon as he had his new rifle ready to shoot and his backpack on, he forgot altogether about life on the other side of the river. A new excitement took hold of him.

"Let's go get 'em, Slim!" he said jubilantly.

Like a couple of soldiers they stalked across the snowy brown grass toward the woods. The forest loomed up before them in the snowy dawn, a wall of trees stripped bare by the cold, hard rain and winds of autumn. There was the crack of a shot somewhere, then another, and Grant felt a rush of adrenaline.

"Hunters!" Slim piped up.

Before entering the woods they agreed to meet at the same spot at noon, and then they set off through the trees in opposite directions. Grant could smell chlorine from the plant not far off and traces of gunpowder. In damp air he knew that smells could linger, particularly as there was hardly a breeze, and he presumed that at some recent time a hunter had been by this way and fired a shot. He tried his best to pad quietly along, but there were twigs everywhere blown down from the rainstorms, and under the bit of snow they were undetectable and snapped under his feet in the heavy silence. He heard the bang of a rifle not far away. The island wasn't very large and he knew how careful hunters had to be lining up shots. Rifles like the one he was toting could fire a bullet a long, long way. He passed slowly through a clearing and here the snow was falling in a thick white shower. He swiped at his tickling nose and eyebrows to brush away the cold flakes that came to rest there. At the edge of the trees on the other side he thought he heard movement. He stopped and stood dead still, raised his silvery rifle and,

inching between the trunks, scanned the woods, his finger on the trigger.

But he saw nothing. It could have been a squirrel, he thought, leaping from one tree to another. Or a rabbit too. He moved forward among the trees, so far away it seemed from civilization. It was such a pleasant escape from his claustrophobic and humdrum life—stuck in a garage by day and wrapped up in a box of an apartment by night. He heard a shot off somewhere. Quite a way, he told himself. The next shot cracked out like a clap of thunder and he knew it was much closer.

He stopped and stood still. He wouldn't move on, not for a bit, not with that. He stood his rifle up against the wet bark of a tree, slipped off his backpack, and took out a cigarette. He lit it with a lighter that Slim and his wife had bought for him for his birthday. It was engraved with his name and the date, April I. He knew that Carol had bought it and not Slim. Men, especially Slim, did not look for birthday presents. As he stood there smoking, the smoke hanging over him in amorphous little clouds before slowly floating upwards into the bare, gnarled, dripping branches of the trees, he reminisced fondly about Carol. She was a plump redhead with curly hair and big blue eyes. She was buxom and well-proportioned and he'd thoroughly loved the several times they'd gotten together. She wanted it to be an ongoing thing but he'd told her he didn't think it was a good idea, sooner or later they'd get caught. Still, they were going to meet again next week.

For a moment he'd forgotten where he was, until a shot cracked out nearby and a whining bullet sliced a furrow across the side of a tree trunk not ten feet away. He snapped his head around but couldn't see a deer anywhere. Then he saw Slim come loping toward him.

Panting, he said, "I saw a buck movie' through!" Locks of dishevelled hair hung down over his forehead and his eye like ragged slips of cloth. "You musta bin behind a tree, b'Jesus! I never woulda shot if Fda known, Grant."

"It's okay," Grant said, unnerved. "It must've been real close to me."

Slim lit up a cigarette and they stood there in the stillness of the woods. The snow seemed to be letting up.

"How many guns d'ya think there are?"

"Who knows?" said Grant. He was uneasy; the impact of what had happened was beginning to make itself felt. He realized he could be lying dead on the ground. "As the morning goes on there'll be more hunters. Some don't like gettin' out o' bed early."

It was daylight now and Grant told himself it would be safer. Next year he wouldn't be coming out in the darkness of dawn. He could hear seagulls squawking in the distance and, a minute later, the nettled screech of a blue jay. He glanced around but couldn't spot it. He was sick of the cigarette and flicked it on the ground, squishing it into smithereens with his heavy boot.

"I'm going," he told Slim, and put on the backpack. He picked up his rifle. "I'll see you at noon."

Slim watched his pal walk away. Not *'pal'* anymore, that was for sure! They'd been such good friends. Standing there smoking, he asked himself how a man could be buddies with someone going to bed with his wife. He wasn't stupid. Maybe he hadn't gone to school long but he wasn't dumb. Not this Slim boy here, no way! He sneered at Grant. You fuckin' bastard! he thought. He drew heavily on the cigarette and blew out the smoke like a pent-up bellows. All he could see in his rage was Carol straddling him, his supposed pal. Back and forth she'd rocked while he stood there in the hall peeping through the crack in the doorway of *'their'* bedroom in *'their'* house. The fucking nerve of 'em! He could still hear her moans and sighs, loud as a storm in his ears, and the throaty exchange of words as they approached the end. He still did not know how he'd kept himself from barging in and beating the living daylights out of them. He pushed the butt of his cigarette into the tree and set off the way Grant had gone. "B'Jesus," he said out loud, " I wonder if the bastard knows!"

Agatha was having a busy day. It seemed that no sooner did she restock an item than most of it was gone. Cello packages of spinach disappeared the fastest, on sale as it was for ninety-nine cents. It was a good thing too because she didn't want to come in Monday and face leftovers. Spinach did not keep. As soon as the packages lost their spongy texture, the green leaves leaves started to get slimy. Just past two in the afternoon her attention was drawn to the front of the store where two policemen were talking to Mr. Jardin, the owner. It looked like something serious because they were all glum. She panicked when she saw them look her way and Mr. Jardin pointing too. What was going on?she wondered. Her mind raced. As the policemen came toward her she grabbed hold of the counter. She had an awful feeling and felt faint. She hoped with all her racing heart it wasn't Tamara. Or even Grant.

The policemen were young. One was blond with a scar on his chin and the other had a brushcut and the look of a bulldog but with a glimmer of kindness in his brown eyes.

"Can we go somewhere to talk?" asked the one gravely.

The rest was a blur. All she knew was that a moment later they were sitting in the lunchroom and the policeman with the scar, frowning at her across the table and looking empathetic, said, "There's no way of making this easy, Mrs. Race. Your husband has died in a hunting accident."

She heard the words but they didn't register. She had to analyze them, verify who was speaking. And then her eyes widened in horror and she didn't quite see the two men there with her in their blue garb. Her blood ran cold.

She spent the next two days in a whirlwind of interaction with others while the events seemed altogether out of her control. It was as if they were being managed by an invisible, powerful force, pulling her along helplessly willy-nilly. There were phone calls expressing sorrow, people she ran into who'd heard, and there was Tamara. Tamara refused to believe it at first. She'd fled to her room and closed the door and Agatha had heard her sobbing for a long time. There was the visit to the funeral home to pick out the casket. Thankfully, the man there was going to get the plot in the cemetery, take care of contacting the newspaper and putting in the obituary. She gave him the details across a lovely oak desk with a glass-covered top and a vase of red carnations off to the side. The office was warm and inviting, and redolent of flower scents from an air freshener. Off through the panes of the window she could see the traffic moving along the street. It all seemed like just another routine, making the arrangements, something like going to the grocery store or the dentist, a part of life, nothing unusual at all, a defeat and a graceful capitulation, an acknowledgment of mortality.

Luckily she could use a credit card. She had no money, nor had Grant. Save for a couple of hundred dollars in his savings account. Though he had some life insurance through his work.

They all came to see him, some in the afternoon and some in the evening. With Tamara by her side, she stood there in her good red suit accepting hugs and kisses from friends and relatives. She never realized they knew so many people. It evolved into a social gathering of sorts so that momentarily, from time to time, she tended to forget where she was. It occurred to her that it was a little like a wedding or a New Year's Eve party but with grave undertones. Tamara, she could tell, was not taking any of it too well. She really loved her father. She seemed even paler, her eyes clearly red. Agatha was glad Ethan was at her side. He would reach out occasionally and stroke her back during harder times. They seemed almost like man and wife, quite suited to each other, making her wonder if they would eventually get married. She'd worn her charm bracelet and whenever she moved her arm it tinkled. She hated to admit that none of her good luck charms had done much yet to make her life any easier. Still, she believed in them. They held a certain fascination for her, that was all that mattered. They offered a ray of hope. Perhaps. Just perhaps.

The grandparents took it all in stride. They sat quietly on a green brocade sofa behind Tamara and herself. They were like statues, Agatha thought, quiet and never heard from. Death seemed to be irrelevant. Most of their friends were gone after all and they were probably used to it. They'd seen them away just like this, in a parlor where the dead person lay in a fancy box lined with satin, bordered with ruffles. She gazed at Grant now and again. He was just as handsome as the day they'd met. He seemed about ready to climb out of that shiny wooden casket and walk away. She couldn't believe it, any of it. The bullet had gone clear through him, killing him instantly. Just a little hole, she imagined. That was what had ended it all. That was why everybody was here. Her life seemed spoiled entirely. She felt happiness was for someone else, certainly now It would not be easy going on. She was glad of Tamara, glad of her daughter. She was by her side and would be there back at home too. It took off some of the rough edge.

The funeral was a somber affair. There was a short service in the funeral home conducted by a minister whom Agatha did not know. It was somewhat consoling for everyone to think, even if only momentarily, that Grant was in a better place. That was the slant of the minister's words. Agatha believed it because she believed there was a god. She and Tamara were led out in front of a solemn throng of people to the motorcade of waiting cars and, with the grandparents, got into a long black limousine. A short time later she watched the pallbearers, all Grant's friends, carry out the casket and load it into the back of the hearse. Somehow she was beginning to feel better. She clasped Tamara's hand.

The ride to the cemetery along the quiet city streets seemed to take forever. Agatha wished it was all over with and she was back home, or even at work. One more hurdle, she thought. One more and all of it will come to an end.

The day's warmth was such a change and she noticed that the snow was all but gone, melted into the ground. Like Grant would soon be too. It *was* an odd way of thinking but she could not help herself. As she sat next to the grave, a green blanket underfoot, she hardly lifted her eyes off the casket. She held Tamara's hand while Ethan stood behind, the remaining entourage encircling the canvas gazebo as if to get a first hand look at something forbidden, something secret that the rest of the world shouldn't see. She was thinking how element it was for the time of year and about her job. She was off for a few days.

And she was thinking too about Nathan and shamefully some of the things she could do now that Grant was…well, where he was, there, only a few feet away, forever in a box. Grant had been okay at times but really their marriage had been a sham. It had to do with money of course and his drinking and, she had to admit, her gambling. But he'd hardly been nice to her except for going to work every day and bringing home a pay check. He was reliable that way. And she thought he'd been mostly faithful but who could ever know for sure about a thing like that?

The minister reeled off his spiel, a Bible reading, psalms because they were so lachrymose, and she cried a little because of the words, hardly for any other reason. But Tamara carried on, very open with her sobbing and her tears, and all she could do was squeeze her daughter's hand as if to say, "It's okay, it's nearly over."

When everything was all said and done, the minister plucked the small cross off the casket and handed it to Agatha.

"Thank you," she said.

"He's with God." And he placed his hand on her shoulder.

Agatha was hard at work setting up her produce displays when Nathan sidled up beside her. She was lining up fresh bunches of green onions in a tray like perfect little soldiers when she felt someone's touch.

"Darn, you scared me!" she exclaimed with a start, smiling.

"I'm sorry, Aggy," Nathan told her. "About your husband."

"I know," she said. "My daughter feels quite bad. It's going to take a while."

"Would yuh like tuh go for a coffee, maybe later?"

She hesitated, looked at the floor where a red elastic lay beside her shoe. She didn't know, she just didn't know. Deep down she wanted to but it probably wouldn't look right given the timing. "When?" she found the deepest part of herself asking.

"Nothin' wrong with tonight."

"Okay," she said.

"I'll come and get you at eight."

"Not my place, no." She was thinking of Tamara. "I'll meet *you...* " She thought quickly. "The bus stop. There on the corner. Down this way from the apartment"

"I'll be there."

He touched her hand with his and walked away.

She spent the rest of the day with her mind mostly on Nathan. She could not deny herself this. He was good looking, very 'cute', with a broad smile and deep dimples at the sides of his mouth. He *was* tall too and well-built, with broad shoulders. She did not really owe her husband any post mortem loyalty. She'd put up with his alcohol-fueled bursts of anger for a long time. What did it matter to anyone, except Tamara, that she was seeing someone so close on the heels of her husband's death? She would keep it a secret, at least for a while.

They went to a coffee shop in a nearby town, and then drove back to where Nathan had taken her before. She didn't feel as guilty about it as she had the last time. She was single now and her only remorse was that Tamara would not approve. They sat in the darkness of the car discussing everything. Agatha could tell, even if she hadn't known him, had never seen him before, that he was quite a bit younger than herself. It was the upbeat and optimistic tone of his voice, his zest for life that came out in everything he said. He'd never had, as far as she knew, any major tragedies to deal with or obligations with regard to a family of his own. He drove a nice car and lived at home and, she presumed, all he made working at the store he saved or spent on himself. She was envious.

"I get that yuh feel guilty," he said. "But yuh got your own life. Yuh got tuh live your own life, girl. It doesn't matter what other people say. Just do your own thing."

"It's Tamara not me."

"Sure," he said.

They kissed and things quickly reached the point where he suggested "going somewhere." In the heat of it all, she agreed, having conveniently tucked away all her qualms to satisfy a longstanding lust. She tried not to think of anything as the car sped out of town along the dark hilly road beside the creek. The blackness of night was everywhere, invasive, even into her mind. But she would not give in to negative or gloomy thoughts. She was going to enjoy this, she was determined no matter. She reached over and put her hand on Nathan's back and felt an unusual and pleasant sort of lethargy come over her. She closed her eyes and the thrum of the motor quickly lulled her into a state of helpless

torpor.

"We're here, Aggy," she heard someone say.

Her eyes fluttered open and she gasped for breath. She realized she'd fallen asleep! She saw they were at a motel, a small one, and down along in front of the rooms there was not a car.

"I'll be right back," he said, getting out.

He left the door ajar and the cold air rushed in at her. She shivered, embracing herself. Sex, she thought, without mincing words, raw sex. The secrecy of it all, the forbidden fruit, the darkness, the gaudy neon that read 'Motel', and, most of all, a new lover! She felt a tingle and a rush of anticipation. Her mind was steamy with hot salacious thoughts.

Room nine. It was down near the end by the empty swimming pool. Nathan pulled up in front of the door, which, she noticed, looked freshly painted, as did the window sashes. She could tell it was an older motel. It had a worn, yet well cared for look.

Stepping inside, Nathan flipped on the light and she could see in a flash that things were neat and clean. The room smelt like evergreen. Nathan didn't give her time even to take off her coat. He put his hands on her shoulders and turned her right around to face him and, pausing first to gaze down at her with those lovable dark eyes of his, placed his warm lips on hers. She closed her eyes, feeling herself melting into him.

He was not shy, she could tell. He removed all his clothes and then hers, whispering about what he was going to do to her. They got into bed and slid under the floral comforter and she fell into a hot whirlwind of lust and sexual fulfillment.

She began to cry quietly, even before it was over and he lay on his back beside her. It had felt so good and yet she felt so guilty for having done it, though she would not tell him. She had betrayed Tamara and she was sorry.

"What's wrong, Aggy?"

"Nothing," she murmured, stifling a sob. "Pm just maudlin sometimes."

"Upset?"

"It's got nothing to do with you."

She gained control of herself and in the dark room, with only wisps of light slipping in from outside, she listened to Nathan's breathing. She could feel his hotness there beside her. She needed to hold him in the chill. She turned on her side and laid an arm on his chest. A heavy sense of loneliness weighed down on her. Though she mostly hadn't loved Grant, she was going to be alone and might miss him for only that reason. There would be no one there, aside from Tamara, who seemed rarely to be home anymore. A troubling cluster of concerns and worries made her feel anxious. How was she going to cope? How was she ever going to look after all the things?

Nathan dropped her off a short way from her apartment and drove slowly home thinking about the evening. Aggy was definitely a 'keeper'. She wasn't gorgeous but attractive, perfectly plump with full breasts. He tingled all over. She was just what he needed, for the time being anyhow. He knew it could not be permanent because when he married, if ever, he wanted a younger wife. He did like Agatha, however, as a friend. She was very nice, with a kind, sweet personality. He saw it as the beginning of an affair. She seemed still married and that made it all the more tantalizing. Pulling into the long driveway, he began to plot their next rendez-vous.

Chapter Six

Ethan was with his friend when the snow began. They were sitting in a quiet little bar not far from the school. Alec had his own car, a sharp-looking but older BMW, which he kept immaculate. Ethan could honestly not remember the last time he'd seen it dirty. Even now, as he gazed out at it through the small snowflakes gently floating down, it displayed a flashy sheen. The car was just like its owner, Ethan smiled. Alec was spotless himself, always clean, always neat, only a little overbearing at times, and a lover of the arts. Ethan admired him.

He said, "I wasn't supposed to tell anyone, I promised her."

Alec, who was broad-shouldered and husky with short blond hair, sounded reassuring. "You know it won't go any further than this." And he pointed at himself. Then he shook his head and frowned. "She should have been on the pill, Ethan. What I can't understand, man, is why not? I know you're smarter than that. What were you thinking? Condoms are okay but, hell, they're not a sure thing!"

Ethan said practically begging for understanding, "She was too embarrassed to ask for pills. She didn't want anybody to know. She said it was okay. She said it would be safe, condoms were all we needed. She said she had it all figured out." He made a slicing motion with his hand for emphasis. "And I damn well believed her! God, you know how beautiful she is!"

Alec drank some beer and set the bottle down hard. Ethan could tell he was riled. "You're goddam well done if you stay in this thing, Ethan. Honest. I'm telling you for your own good. Just think, man! I know you can use that brain of yours. You might never get to be that lawyer I know you want to be. How can you go to school with a wife and a baby? Where will the money come from? Even if you had the money or your mother and father gave it to you or whatever—hell, man, what kind of life would you have at university? You wouldn't be able to go anywhere or see anything or do what you want to do. Life would be miserable. You're a responsible person, I know, man. You'd come out with us to a movie or a concert or whatever and you wouldn't be having a good time because you'd be feeling guilty about leaving her at home with a squalling baby."

Ethan was glum. He took off his glasses and set them on the table and rubbed his eyes. He knew he shouldn't have come here today. Alec was such a strong personality. He did not mince words, saying exactly what he thought. Yet it was this bluster and insistance of his that was so appealing. Ethan found it admirable that someone could be so unabashed and yet also a patron of the arts, a connaisseur of the finer things in life, which are placid and unabrasive and inclined to promoting harmony.

"I know you're right, Alec, and I've been feeling that way. I can't just leave her. I think I love her enough. I'm going to take it one step at a time. One, two, three."

"It's your decision, man." Alec shook his head, sat back, and folded his arms, Ethan thought he looked a little deflated and was maybe searching for a stronger line of dissuasion. "She *is* a looker, I will say that. A lot of guys would like to go out with her. I wouldn't blame you for sticking with her. I just wanted to lay the cards down on the table, man, that's all. The way I see them, if it were me I think I'd split and run."

The waitress came up to the table and Ethan noticed how Alec's face suddenly turned from a piece of rock into a dollop of whipped cream. "We'll have two more," he said with a smile.

Ethan didn't really want another bottle of beer. He would have preferred nursing along what he had left. But he was glad to stay on with his friend. Lately he'd been spending most of his time with Tamara, who was generally feeling terrible. There'd been her father's sudden death and he knew how close she'd been to him, and now this pregnancy. In the last few days she'd suffered through bouts of morning sickness, managing to hide them from her mother.

He noted how the snow was thicker now, falling like a veil. He could hardly see the BMW. That would be one thing he knew he wouldn't be getting for awhile. Not if he stayed with Tamara and saw it all through. He hated thinking about it and could hardly believe it was happening.

"What's up, man? I can see the clockwork spinning around."

"Oh, the weather," Ethan said.

"Yeah, right!"

The waitress, a dark-haired young woman, waltzed over with the beer and Alec paid.

As soon as she was gone, Ethan said, "Hey, that was supposed to be mine. You got the last one." "I'm trying to take care of you, man."

Alec laughed, picked up the bottle of beer, and took a good long drink, sighing after with satisfaction,

"You think I should leave her, don't you?"

"Definitely, Ethan. Definitely, man. You're going to thank me later. Honest. It's what I believe is best for you....But it's your call."

Agatha ate by herself, not sure at all how Tamara was doing. She was only ever home to sleep. Her moods were pu77ling, they seemed to quickly swing one way and then another. She'd always been a quiet, reserved sort of child, though lately, it seemed, she was often short-tempered, as if something was bothering her. And an instant after, she would turn into a smiling, happy, and lovable young woman. It was the death of her father, Agatha surmised, yet she knew Tamara well enough to know there likely was something else. Where had the petulance come from? She'd hardly ever been that way before.

Agatha finished her baked potato and drank some milk. She thought about Nathan. He wanted to see her again, tomorrow night. He said they could go to his place for a while because his parents were going Christmas shopping with his brother James; it would have to be early though, about seven. She'd agreed.

She could hear muffled bits of conversation in the hall and then it faded away. The one thing she did not like about living in an apartmenet building was the hodgepodge of cooking smells that hovered at suppertime. There was a very nice Chinese family two doors down who favored garlic and onions and the pungent odor usually ended up making its wily way into her place.

She couldn't help thinking back on the sex she'd had with Nathan. It had been the best ever but psychologically she was not ready for it. Grant had just died and it didn't seem right. He'd been good to her much of the time and especially to Tamara. It was when he'd gone overboard with his drinking that she'd lost affection for him. She had loved him on and off, she supposed. Now it was Tamara she felt she was cheating.

She cleaned off the table and washed the dishes in the sink, rinsing them off and setting them in the rack to drain. The dishwasher did not work anymore, they'd never replaced it.

And of course money was another thing. There was just never enough.

She left the kitchen and went into the spare bedroom. She put her finger on the acorn beside the computer monitor and, closing her eyes, prayed to God for wealth. Please, she thought, just a little to pay my bills. It would sure be nice! She concentrated so deeply that she managed to become almost semi-conscious. There was only her mind, she no longer had a body, she was spirit far, far away.

The sound of the phone startled her. She snapped out of the trance and picked up the receiver.

It was her mother in Barrie. "Were you busy, Agatha? I know you must be very busy these days what with being alone. It's a terrible burden."

"Mom, never mind all that. How are you?"

"I have a surprise! That's why I called."

"I love surprises."

"Your father and I are going to give you two-thousand dollars to help with the funeral. And Christmas is coming too."

"Mom, that's wonderful!...But you don't have to. You need that money, you and dad."

"We'll be alright. We've talked this over and we want you to have it."

They chatted for a while about everyday things, Christmas, and of course getting together. "Don't forget to say 'Hi' to Tamara for me. Tell her I'll see her then and give her a great big hug."

"I will, mom."

"Good bye, dear."

Agatha couldn't believe it. Sitting in the living-room, she told herself it had to be the acorn: her mother calling and offering money. She needed to believe in magic. Her lucky charms were her little friends. Even when they let her down she knew there was reason.

Tamara came home after one, quietly locked the door, and padded through the dark apartment to her room. She was chilly, just from the short jaunt from the car to the door of the building, and, in the light of a small lamp, she got undressed as fast as she could, slipping into flannel pyjamas. The neatly made bed, with its fluffy comforter and her little family of watchful puppies sitting up along the foot

board, seemed so inviting she just wanted to get in and curl up. Nonetheless, she zipped buoyantly off to the bathroom where she flossed and brushed her teeth, and gargled, swishing around mint mouthwash. She put her hands on her hips and smiled. In the mirror it was nice to see that her teeth were so white. "Try to brush them at least twice a day," the dentist had advised her. She could see it was working. She told herself she was pretty. She only wished that her whole face would smile. She had a sad, serious look that seemed indelible and contrasted sharply with the happy twist of her mouth. Perhaps it's because of my eyes, she thought. They just seemed so deep and pensive, away almost in another world. Well, she did daydream an awful lot and did her share of pondering too. You're so deep, Tamara, she mused, you're deeper than the ocean.

With the lamp on she got into bed and it wasn't long before she was sleepily warm and comfortable. This was her world, this room, and she loved it in here. It represented innocence and she liked to believe it was impervious to misfortune, which could surely never find its way in. It was out there, outside, and in here she was invulnerable. Her father came to mind. Now *he* was one she'd not been able to forget for long. He kept popping up in her mind, like a garden gnome. Her eyes watered. Closing them, she pushed the tears out so that they trickled down by her ears. She would never see him again. Not ever. He would never see her baby either. She placed a hand on her abdomen. She was sure there was a change. Soon, she wouldn't be able to dress in the same clothes. She wondered how long she could hide it, how long before people began to give her sidelong looks, before either her mother asked or she'd have to tell? She was troubled. She wiggled down a little further under the covers as if they could somehow protect her. Ethan though was supportive. When he was around she was sure everything would be fine. He told her they could get through it, none of it would be as bad as she imagined, even revealing the secret. She was a believer. Perhaps that was why everybody considered him a good actor. He really was great on stage, she told herself with a smile. She wondered if he might really become a professional actor or end up a lawyer? Either was fine with her. She didn't like him hanging around with Alec. Alec seemed fond of having a good time and jumping from girl to girl. He never seemed to stick to anyone for long. She could only wonder what Ethan and Alec talked about when they were together. The worst thing that could happen would be for Ethan to abandon her.

Agatha got dressed up in thee black slacks and a red angora sweater, and did her hair and makeup in front of the mirror. She stood back after and gave herself a long look, Red and black were definitely her colors, her long blond hair cascading to her shoulders in contrast. The dark roots of her hair weren't glaringly obvious and she refused to let them detract from the positive opinion she had of herself. She felt she was doing well for thirty-seven. Walking to and from work was enough exercise and she made it a point to eat healthy foods. She must still be attractive, she told herself, if a cute, well-built thirty-two year-old man was interested in her.

She didn't wear a hat and regretted it, striding along a block or so from the apartment. The cold was biting and she hurried her step in her soft winter boots and soon could feel a warm flush in her cheeks. The sidewalks were bare and only icy in spots and she made good time past the older houses and the front yards with their thin icing of snow. She'd of course lied to Tamara about her destination. She didn't like lying certainly but Tamara would not have understood. It was all benign. For now, bingo or the casino would suffice.

Nathan's house was in a cul de sac in an upscale neighborhood where the homes were large and new and the driveways gleaming with expensive cars. Agatha could not imagine where all the money came from. As she approached the house, she could see him waiting inside the door. She had the disturbing notion that she was going somewhere just to get flicked and then would return home. It wasn't fair to think that way of Nathan. She believed his intentions were more noble. After all, what young man didn't enjoy sex?

"Hey, what's up, Aggy? Come on in," he said as she stepped past him into the warmth of the foyer. "You look cold. I wanted tuh pick yuh up."

"I know," she said, taking off her gloves. "It was my decision. Not a problem. I like walking, I'm used to it."

He wanted her to sit down in the living-room and, while he hung up her coat, she padded across the bright hardwood floor to a black leather chair in the corner of the grandiose room. She was awestruck, it was so spectacular! Her eyes moved around like blotters taking everything in. There was a collection of lovely leather furniture in black, red, and tan, and glass tables, and colorful abstract pictures in chrome frames which managed to bring the smoky gray walls to life. Five or six floor lamps with shades in quaint shapes showered subdued light everywhere, even off into the far corners. It was luxurious, warm, and romantic, and she loved it. She wanted to be rich. It was a vicarious moment, utterly thrilling.

He brought her a glass of chilled white wine and set it on a lavender coaster. "There yuh go, girl. Enjoy!"

"Thank you, Nathan."

He had a bottle of beer without a glass and she watched as he swaggered lazily over to a chair. She admired his rugged build. The only thing that bothered her was his age. It could work though, she told herself with some uncertainty. It would be a difficult task however bringing Tamara in on everything. Perhaps in the future, when her grief would no longer be such a factor.

"They won't get back for a while," he said. "After the stores close they're goin' for a bite tuh

eat."

"Oh?" Was that to reassure her they'd have enough time? she wondered. She figured so. "It doesn't matter, Nathan."

"About three hours."

So they had three hours to get the job done, did they? Then she quickly admonished herself for being so cynical.

"Are you going to take over from your father?" she asked.

"The store?"

"Yes."

He pursed his mouth meditatively and after some deliberation said, "It's all set up that way. All I gotta do is ramble on. If somethin' good's handed tuh yuh on a platter, you betcha I'm gonna grab it….Say, Aggy, how you bin getting' along on your own? Everythin' okay?"

She found herself comparing Grant and Nathan. Grant had been more meek, less boastful, though she didn't see Nathan completely as a braggart. He was just younger, more gung-ho about things, positive and less set in his ways. Which wasn't to say Grant was altogether negative. Just more grown up and more mature, that was about it. They were both very good-looking! Nathan was 'cool', and Grant was, well, 'with it' should she say?

"I miss him," she said, without conviction. "One day he was there and the next he was not. I can handle it. It bothers me. If I told you it didn't I would be lying. Tamara sure misses him. She really seems depressed and into herself. I hope she's going to be able to get on with her life and not let this weigh her down forever."

"It'll be okay," Nathan said, stretching his legs. "I betcha in a couple o' months she'll be back tuh normal, Aggy."

"I hope you're right."

They talked about the store and how the place always seemed to be open. Nathan said it was because of all the competition. If one store was open Sundays and holidays they had to be too.

"A vicious circle," she said with a smile.

"You betcha. See, people got no time. Their hands're tied durin' the week. Workin' all day 'n night 'n who knows when. 'N on Sundays, well, they do their shoppin'. My dad says it never was like that before. Sundays were set aside and kept kind o' quiet. Now it's business as usual, Aggy."

The phone rang, startling them, and Nathan picked it right up there where he was sitting. She couldn't help but hear.

"What d'you want?" he asked, sounding put out. "I'm busy, I can't talk right now….I don't care….Look, I'll call yuh later…. None o' your business….It wasn't meant tuh be…."

He hung up, forcefully clunking the receiver into the cradle. She could see by his face there was some kind of problem. He hardly looked happy. She didn't think the phone call had anything to do with the store, more like a former girlfriend he didn't want to bother with. Or was that all an act because she was here? She wasn't going to ask.

He took a good long drink of beer. "Finish it off!" he laughed and then chugged down the rest. "Have another?"

She said, "Yes," automatically.

When he came back with the drinks he sat down again across the way, studying her as he held the bottle of beer in his lap like a genie would a lamp.

"Why did you ask me to come here?" she wamted to know.

He was a bit taken aback and his dark eyebrows popped up in surprise. He tilted his head and gazed at her appraisingly. "You *know* why," he said, melting into his smile of bright white teeth.

"Explain yourself, Nathan." She was smiling wryly.

"You'll see! Now it's my turn for a question....Aggy girl, why in the hell don't you have a driver's licence?"

She laughed and sipped some of the wine. "I have a common sense response: I don't know how to drive and I sure don't have enough money to maintain a car either, or pay for insurance. I'm going to sell the old jalopy. Grant made sure that Tamara got her beginner's though. But she doesn't seem too interested in driving."

"I don't know how the hell anybody can stand not havin' a car!"

"You get used to it," she explained. She glanced at her charm bracelet. Two things: the ace of hearts was facing down and the silver cottage was topsy-turvy. Not good! "My parents are giving me two-thousand dollars to help with the funeral expenses. It was sure a surprise."

"Good for you," he said. He raised his glass. "Cheers!"

She drank to the toast and could feel herself letting go. She was amazed that she was here at all,doing this. She hadn't been brought up to be promiscuous. She was good-looking and quiet, not one to give in very easily. Yet, she'd fallen. Perhaps it was because deep down she was depressed and not willing to deal with things. Death was hard. You did whatever to escape the harsh reality. But the forgetting seldom lasted long.

"Your wheels are tumin', Aggy."

She nodded and gazed down at her weatherbeaten hands. She didn't have the softeness or pretty painted nails other women seemed to flit around with. The requirements of her job were mostly to blame. She always wore gloves on her walks and used moisturizing cream at home too. She'd tried wearing latex gloves at work to handle the icy cold fruit and vegetables but they made things awkward. The little cracks and cuts burned and stung. What she really needed was to go to a spa somewhere in a warm climate. Like the ads she saw in magazines. *That* would be nice, though she knew it was out of the question.

They drank some more and he came over and took her hand, not saying a thing, suggesting by his gentle tug that she get up. Lust was written all over his face. She felt herself melting, giving in. As wrong as she knew it was she couldn't resist.

Later on at home in bed she reminisced. The portable TV was barely audible, flashing every now and again as scenes changed. She wasn't paying much attention to it save for a vacant gaze as her mind pored over other things. He wouldn't let her walk home. He'd made her take a ride, every bit the gentleman. He'd opened and closed the doors for her and regretted having to drop her off a way from the apartment. Still, despite his attentions and kindness she knew it was all for fun. She couldn't foresee any sort of commitment either way. It just was not practical. She supposed it didn't matter anyhow. She was hardly ready for heady things. Though it would have been gratifying, still, to feel she was not being used. Perhaps it was just her. Maybe his intentions *were* noble.

It was eery seeing her wedding photo there on the wall beside the dresser. In the slate-colored glow of the TV, there they were, Grant and herself, she in her white gown and he in his tuxedo. Anyonecould tell he wasn't comfortable in formal attire. He resembled a mannequin. He didn't seem so horrible now in retrospect, a good-looking guy who drank too much. Didn't they all have some weakness or other? Tears welled into her eyes. She missed him in the more favorable light of hindsight. She believed he did love her. There'd been times when she'd been passionate about him too. But what difference did it all make now? She was alone, poor, with a daughter to raise—and carrying on with her employer's son. It was depressing stuff.

A week passed and on Sunday, just after lunch, Ethan came to pick up Tamara. He was driving his father's Mercedes, a car he loved and one Tamara enjoyed riding in. It made him feel immense. People looked, he knew they did, and that was a thrill. He waited for Tamara in the parking lot. The snow had melted and there were scattered puddles. He saw no sense in getting out and blotching his shiny black shoes.

Tamara was a charm, a real sweety pie, he thought with regret. But what choice was there? He saw her come out and watched as she walked towards the car. Her lovely oval face was like a cameo framed with her long black hair, and her legs seemed extra long today in sharp black dress slacks. She'd been satsifying in bed, having gotten to know what pleased him and vice versa. But most recently there'd been none of that. Just because she was pregnant. He knew the facts. There would be no harm.

It angered him.

"Hi, Ethan," she said, getting into the car. She kissed him on the cheek, leaving a lipstick image. "I can hardly believe how warm it is. I don't know why I even wore the coat."

In a moment they were off. He didn't have much to say, only that it was easy to get around because the roads were dry and a few words on the upcoming Christmas play. He was taking the part.

She protested mildly. "Ethan you told me you weren't. You said it would take up too much

time."

"I know," was all he said. There was only quiet as the car purred along. He felt guilty not telling her, he was afraid. Hescuttled it to the back of his mind, glancing at things going by. It would have been difficult to tell that Christmas was only a couple of weeks away, he mused, if it weren't for the

decorations. The grass was actually green everywhere, having lost its tawny autumnal dinginess, the snow having brought it back to life. It

was even mild enough to play golf. The Yule decorations seemed to him to be out of time and place, stark strangers lost across the

springlike landscape. He noticed snowmen and candy canes up on the light posts, and here and there a lawn Santa Claus looking lonely and

forlorn.

"How come you're so quiet?" she wanted to know.

"I was just daydreaming is all….What would you like for Christmas?"

She considered for a moment, smiled sheepishly, and whispered, "You!"

His sentimental side wanted to reach out and embrace the idea of her love in a longlasting relationship. His crueler, selfish one refused. It was protective covering, like a roof on a house or wax on a car. He cowered inside, still managing to smile and wink at her with a beam of affection. It wasn't long before they got to the big gray building down by the bridge. There was an orange and red sign up near the roof that said Tropical Birds. He parked in the back in the crowded lot and got out of the car. He stretched his arms and took a deep breath in an effort to relax. Tamara was calling him, gesturing for him to come around and open her door. She was a real pain at times! he thought.

The bird sanctuary was quite an escape, at least that was how Ethan saw it, magnificent, lush, and imposing, with plants and shrubs and trees giving the illusion of being piled on top of one another all the way up to the ceiling, where large fans whirred lazily round and round. He seized Tamara's hand and pulled her along enthusiastically.

Gazing at an Everglades velvetseed flecked with creamy white flowers, he said, "This is definitely a tropical tree." No sooner had he made the remark than a rainbow lorikeet hopped out from between the branches. "There! There! Look! Blue and red and yellow and green."

"Tropical birds are *so* pretty!" she exclaimed.

The forest was secured by a mesh screen. The building was somewhat humid, for the needs of the avian population, and an earthy smell

hung in the air. The multifarious birdsongs intermingled with one another making for a continual cacophony that, though sweet and

innocent enough, could, after a time, set one's nerves on edge. Ethan saw a couple parrots, both bright blue, bop out of a tangle of liana

and fly up into the crown of a royal palm, disappearing among the fronds.

"Well?"

"It's wonderful," Tamara said, looking into his perceptive eyes. "I wanted to come here today because I've never been and because I wanted a change from the sad dark weather. It's odd how it's so happy in here and out there in the world it drains you. It's gray and depressing. When it's like that it takes the life out of you. I wanted to see green again. I wanted to see happiness. I wanted to listen to all the birdsSometimes I feel so lonely I can hardly stand it, Ethan. I don't know why though. I have you, I know that. But I get these horrible all alone feelings." She lowered her head as they stood there beside a window facing each other while people shuffled by in awe of the colorful birds. "Do you really love me, Ethan?"

He placed his hands on her shoulders and looked as sincere as he could. "What do you think? Of course I do!" He did love her, he knew that, or at least he thought that was what it was. He rallied Shakespeare: "'You are a dish fit for the gods.'"

She slugged him playfully. "So are you!" And she stormed away with a burst of laughter.

They shuffled up and down the paths with the rest of the people, not saying much at all, in awe of the beauty and the colors. Atop a manchineel shrub a hummingbird hovered, no bigger than a large bee, bluish green, turning into a dart as it fired off and disappeared somewhere up in the foliage.

"Wow!" exclaimed Ethan.

"I glimpsed it barely."

"They're so so fast!"

They bought soft drinks and then sat on the patio at a small table tucked away among ornamental trees.

"Why did did you take the part?" she protested petulantly. "I said it might not be a good idea. Acting takes a lot of time, Ethan. I need you more than ever." She glanced down at her stomach. "This is ***our*** project—not mine. I want you ***around,*** not off somewhere reciting silly little lines."

So she was on him again, was she? He decided to retort with a bit of mockery. "'I'll not budge an inch,' he said seriously and, "'To thine own self be true.'"

"Stop it!" she chided. "Stop it now!" Her face clearly displayed exasperation. "I can hardly stand it anymore," she sighed, "you and your quotes. Please, get real! You've changed. What's happened to you? You seem like you don't care. It's terrible. You have to be serious....I just don't know. God, I do not know!"

She lowered her head and held it in her hands as if searching for something in her cup. She was right and he knew it.

Chapter Seven

A month passed and the weather was bad, hard winter having set in with biting cold and gusty winds. There was snow enough, especially at the edges of the parking lots, where plows had shoved it up into big banks, and along the sides of the driveways. In places though there were patches of grass, the blades frozen stif and everywhere sheets of hard, stubborn ice. It was like the Arctic. Cars were reluctant to start and some did not, including newer ones, after a night out in bone-numbing, frigid temperatures. The few people who happened to be walking anywhere, or rather shuffling along because of the ice, only reluctantly raised their heads out of the warm folds of their scarves and coats to acknowledge another passerby. It seemed as if there were a plague.

Agatha was moping about the drafty apartment with a nasty cold and a case of the shivers. She just couldn't get warm. She looked a mess but could not have cared less. She was nestled in a corner of the old sofa with her legs curled up, sniffling as she leafed through the magazine. Her blond hair was scraggly, strands of it hanging down over her eyes and face. She was wearing a pink terrycloth housecoat that had known better days, smooth at the elbows where the material had worn away and stained elsewhere from past spills, but washer clean. She had on a sweatshirt and a pair of baggy black sweat pants, and, though her feet were swaddled in good thick socks and ensconced in flannel-lined slippers, her toes stayed cold. She would wiggle them from time to time to get the blood circulating but to no avail. A box of kleenex waited nearby, much of it gone, crumpled up in a pile on the sofa. The radio played soft music and, not only did she find it soothing but it reminded her too that there was still a world out there, even in the cold bluster of winter. She was definitely not alone.

Leafing through the magazine, she pursed her lips in envy at the pictures of happy families, smiling at her with bright cheery faces and lovely white teeth. Could life *really* be like that? she wondered. She supposed, but it hardly seemed in the cards for her. At least not yet. She kept a vase on the floor next to the sofa and in it was a sheaf of fluffy blue peacock feathers, which she would often graze with the tips of her fingers. They were supposed to bring good luck. Noting a picture of a young woman in the magazine with a pale beautiful face and long black hair, she lifted her head and gazed across the room vacantly, thinking about Tamara.

Now there was a girl with a problem. She was pregnant as could be and it was obvious. The news had almost bowled her over. But she'd not let on. Outwardly she'd remained positive, offering encouragement and hugs. But she'd had a terrible dizzy spell at the store and had to come home. She'd taken another couple of days of and gotten a prescription from the doctor at a walk-in clinic. She was going to be a grandmother, which was the only good part. Tamara was struggling and her heart went out to her. She still went to school day after day and carried on the best she could, studying for tests and doing her projects and getting very good marks. But there was morning nausea, and considerable self-consciousness and shame from trying to hide the reality from other kids. But camouflaging it was impossible and Tamara knew it, having abandoned most of the ruses of concealment regarding attire. She wasn't flaunting her condition either, rather beginning not to care. She'd gotten a dsipensation from

phys.ed., though missing something like that, as popular as she was, was in itself suggestive enough to everyone else.

Agatha heard stirrings in the bedroom and knew Tamara was up. She closed the magazine and set it down beside her. Reflecting, she flirted with the peacock feathers. Tamara didn't stay out late on weekends anymore and on school days usually came home and lay down for a while. The pregnancy was taking its toll. Meals were touch and go, with breakfast sometimes missed entirely, but certainly made up for at supper when she ate more than her fill. She recalled the night her daughter came home in a state of shock. Her beautiful black hair was all in a tangle, her eyes red from the tears, and her makeup had run, giving her the pathetic look of a heartbroken raccoon. When she'd asked what was wrong, all Tamara said was, "He's left me, mom," and fled to her room in tears. Agatha remembered opening the bedroom door later and asking to come in. Tamara was sitting on the edge of the bed, and she went over and hugged het What was there to say? It seemed premature, the wound so fresh, but the obvious question, "Why?" came out in a whisper.

The wind had picked up and begun to howl around the building. The screens in the window began to clack like castanets. Agatha looked outside to a blustery day. The bare tree across the way could have been a skeleton hiding in the fog. The snow, in itsy bitsy flakes, like a spray of dust, was gusting down diagonally, making for a ripply sort of haze. Who would go out in this? she wondered. Her head throbbed, even her teeth ached, and her joints were sore too. She'd tried not to think of the mess they were in but it wasn't easy, a tangle of misfortunes and problems that seemed to know no end. Some were financial, many were not. The emotional ones, the ones that had to do with people and relationships, were just as difficult to resolve but at least could be deferred. They hurt certainly but sure didn't put you out on the street. She was behind on the bills. She just was not making enough money. And Tamara, in her condition, certainly couldn't be expected to go out and get work. She wagged her head disconsolately. There seemed to be no solution. Tamara was more important than anything else. She would have to be taken care of, the baby too, and when all of that was done she'd see. There had to be a way out of this quagmire. She would find it. She was determined come hell or high water. At least with Grant around, she thought, though it was a struggle, the bills had gotten paid. There'd been a price however: having to live in apprehension. What was he going to do tonight? Was he going to come home for supper or was he going out drinking? What would he be like when he got back? She'd been the one to bear the brunt of all his frustrations. And would have willingly had he been at least a little more considerate and kind.

Tamara came out into the living-room. Her hair was combed but dull and Agatha thought she looked older than her sixteen years. She had no makeup on which didn't help and her face had taken on a grayish pallor. She wasn't getting out enough, or so Agatha believed, which might account for her unhealthy color. Why, she hardly left the apartment anymore except to go to school. She knew from her own experience that being inside too much led to troubling thoughts and a sense of despondency. But she was tired of making suggestions and didn't feel well enough today to broach the subject. Tamara nonetheless had been seeing her doctor regularly and it was comforting at least to know everything was okay.

"Hi, mom."

"How're you feeling?"

"How's the cold?"

"A little better. I'm probably going to go to work tomorrow. I sure can't afford to sit here for long….I'll get you something to eat."

Tamara waved it off. "It's okay, I can take care of it."

Agatha got right up and went to the kitchen. In a few minutes they were sitting at the table.

"I love toast with honey," Tamara said with a smile. Her mom was just so nice and it was helping a lot. "I could have this at every meal. Dad loved it, I remember."

"You're sort of having your three meals rolled into one today! This is the latest I think you've ever got up."

"I wasn't really sleeping. Just lying there and daydreaming."

"Hey, it's Sunday, Tamara! You can do what you want." Agatha drank leftover coffee heated in the microwave and it was bitter from sitting around. "I should've thrown this out. It's hot at least which is what you want on a day like this." Watching Tamara eating her toast, she was pondering the two of them doing something together like going to a movie or strolling around the mall. She wondered with a twinge if she could afford it and decided barely, perhaps. "Say, would you like to get the heck out of here for a couple hours?"

Tamara gawked at her mom incredulously. It was terrible outside! What was she thinking? "It's pretty stormy."

"What difference does it make? We'll be together, won't we? That's cool enough for sure. When are we going to have another chance? You have to say yes! You have to! We'll take the bus!

The bus is warm. We'll hardly be out at all. We can go to the mall and see what's going on. How's that? I'll buy you some hot chocolate in the little food court."

They were in the mall at about half past four. Tamara felt a new sense of hope as she strolled across the shiny floor beside her mother, who, she knew, was her very best friend. She'd accepted the news of the baby with open arms, not finding fault at all or blaming anyone. There'd been a brief moment of utter surprise of course when her eyes had popped open and her jaw had dropped but that was all. There'd been no harsh words. Just, "Wow, Tamara! I wasn't expecting ***that!*** You'll do well, dear, I'll help you. be there for you." And they'd hugged in tears, the two of them, sobbing quietly there in the kitchen late at night.

The mall was not busy, as it was after Christmas, late Sunday, near closing time, and the rush was over. The Christmas decorations and all the bright lights were still wonderful enough and Tamara felt uplifted. She checked out all the lovely window displays, peering in longer at things she especially admired. But she avoided men's shops, hurrying right on past. She hated Ethan and, at the moment, had a certain loathing for men and all things male. He'd left her flat, he had, all by herself, to have and then raise *his* baby. The wound was still fresh and it seemed that it might never heal. She'd loved him and believed he'd loved her. But she'd been wrong. He was just another young man to her now, chasing a career, looking for fun, valuing freedom and ready to trample anything that got in his way. He wanted to play, as she saw it, but didn't want to pay.

They stepped into a clothing store and headed straight for the dresses. Tamara watched her mom riffle through a rack of them, caressing each one as if to become better acquainted. She knew she couldn't afford them. Why, they barely had enough money for rent. It was a sore topic and she hated thinking about it. If only there was something she could do!

They went into a shoe shop, the lighting pouring down bright beams on the shelves where the lovely new shoes shone in neat quiet pairs. Tamara loved the leather smell. She loved anything good, the same as her mom, who was poring over a pair of brown walkers.

"These would be good," she said, wistfully inching away from them. "They'd be nice-looking and comfortable too."

In the jewellery shop an older woman in a plaid dress pulled out a ruby ring for Agatha to look at. The ring was in white gold, the ruby large, surrounded by scintillating little diamonds.

"I love it, Tamara. I just love it."

Tamara wondered when her mom would ever get to wear it. She only seemed to go to work and come home. Never were there any social events on her calendar. She supposed it was a momentary whim, wanting something merely for the prestige, a treasure to cherish periodically.

They wandered around some more, down this way and back, and then down the next, spending a good halfhour in a book store. They sat for a while too on a bench by a circular flower garden where lush yellow sprays of alyssum, blue gentiana, and pink phlox mingled cozily with strands of greenery in the form of spiked aloe, leafy dieffenbachia and tallish philodendron. They watched people going by, only a few now in dribbles, gawking every which way like lost sheep. Tamara could see out the set of doors that it was pitch black. Car lights, like bug eyes, moved about in the parking lot. She sniffed at the carnival smell of hamburgers and French fries and pizza and Chinese food coming from the food court.

"I think have that hot chocolate, mom," she said. "And a chocolate cookie too."

"Cool," her mother said, and got up, clutching the little brown purse. "I'll have the same. We could use a little sweetness. C'mon."

They had no trouble finding a table. Some workers already were busy cleaning things up for the next morning, most of them young, Tamara saw, figuring they probably went to school all week. A blond boy about her own age was going around wiping down the tables and sweeping up. Aside from herself and her mom, there were only two other people in the food court and they were on the other side eating submarines. The man was fat but looked happy; his wife, however, didn't, and sat there glumly chewing as if it was her last meal. Tamara wondered if two people could be happy together. She'd been. With Ethan. For as long as it had lasted. She didn't think her mom had, with her dad. But that did not impact on her love for her father. He'd always been there for her, kind, backing her in everything, encouraging her to do well in school and get a good education. Tears welled into her eyes. It was all so sad.

"What's wrong?" her mom wanted to know.

"Just the mother thing," she lied. "My moods. I'm fine though."

They sipped away at their hot chocolate, nibbling meantime on the large cookies, meals almost in themselves. Agatha wanted to know about last night.

"We went for Chinese food. Ella paid for everything. Her dad is so good to her."

"He has a profession," Agatha parried. "And her mother works, doesn't she?"

"At the liquor store."

"Money is likely not a problem!"

"Ella laughed the whole time. Well…we went for a drink. I know I shouldn't have but I did. Only one, and then a couple of Cokes too. I

would never harm the baby. The club was busy, A lot of the kids were there…."

"They serve them underage?"

"Sometimes. If there's a big crowd and they're busy. They don't always check ID." "Really?"

"Yeah….It's not so bad. Everybody drinks anyhow. Their older brothers and sisters buy it for them whenever there's a party. You know that!"

Agatha wagged her head. Her face puckered and she sneezed out loud. Dabbing at her nose with a kleenex, she said, "Was Ethan there?"

"No. Uh uh. Good thing too."

"Don't even mention his name, Tamara! It makes me so darn angry to think…"

"I know, I know!" Tamara said, brushing it off. "I've heard it so often before….Anyhow we went for Chinese food then. It was so good! I've got to learn how to make it so it tastes the same as the restaurant….Ella told me she's got a boyfriend. She's so secretive about guys. She wouldn't tell me who he was. I pleaded with her but she wouldn't. She only said she'd just met him a little while ago and that he was tall, dark, and handsome….She's going to become a stewardess and travel around the world. It sounds wonderful. I wouldn't mind that myself."

Agatha shook her head. Tamara was still thinking like a little girl. The woman in her would have to totally emerge for motherhood. "I sure don't think you'll be able to go flying around for a while. Perhaps later."

"Is it the end of the world, mom?"

"It should be the beginning."

They caught the bus outside the doors of the mall. The ride back to the apartment was a warm enough one but rough, and the windows of the bus, splattered brown from road slush, made it difficult to see things clearly. Agatha was glad they'd gone out. Tamara seemed to have had a good time, having been more talkative, and even she herself had benefitted from the jaunt. Her cold was sapping her of energy and now she was definitely ready for bed.

After Tamara had gone to school the next morning, Agatha stood in the living-room with a cup of coffee. The small artificial Christmas tree they'd set up on a red cloth looked sad there in the early light. Christmas was over for another year and there was a sort of letdown. The few presents she and Tamara had exchanged were under the tree, opened, and one of the cards (there'd been very few) had fallen off a branch and was lying open on the floor like a dying bird. She glanced at her charm bracelet. The ace of hearts was staring at her. She hadn't expected it. The household seemed to be in the grip of misfortune. Perhaps luck was about to change. Tamara had left in good spirits, that was encouraging. She took a drink of coffee and peered outside. She expected to see a lot more snow the way it had been blowing but she supposed that the wind had made it sound worse. She'd heard the plows scraping noisily by in the night, the flashes from their blue strobe lights bouncing off the ceiling of her bedroom like silent heartbeats. Dwarfed banks of snow ran up and down either side of the street, but out in the yard the howling wind had blown the snow into smooth drifts several feet high that resembled arrowheads. The walk to work would probably be bone-chilling.

At ten to nine she was already out of her winter things and looking the shelves over. They'd obviously done a good business. Even the cabbage, a product that could hardly be called a great seller, was mostly gone. She was amazed. Perhaps some restaurant had come and bought a pile. That was the most likely explanation. There was not a head of cauliflour left either and only three bunches of brocolli. The carrot display was still intact (another poor seller), the two-pound cello packages in a ragged pile. She noticed a couple of price tags on the floor that no one had bothered to pick up. Her perceptive eyes scanning the field of shelves, she could see there was plenty of work. Each and every item either needed restocking or tidying up. She knew how important appearance was.

She'd already seen Nathan but he'd largely ignored her. He came over a little after eleven to talk. She was busy taking large navel oranges out of a box and lining them up in neat rows.

"Hey, what's up, Aggy? Nice tuh see yuh again!"

"I've been home with a darn cold," she lamented, shaking her head and avoiding his eyes. "I feel a little better today."

"I'm glad, yeah….Sure freezin' out, ain't it?"

"It's January. In a few weeks it'll warm up."

"Not that soon!"

"Okay, March."

"Right now's a good time tuh ramble on down south….Hey, I met your daughter."

Agatha stopped what she was doing and stared into his dark, irresistible, fall-for-him instantly eyes. "Where?"

"At a little bar," he said. "She was as quiet as a mouse. Nice girl!"

"She is," said Agatha curtly. Her face flushed with anger and she trembled. The thought of him near her daughter made her cringe.

"Her friend Ella's pretty friendly."

"She has a boyfriend. She's too young."

Nathan tipped his head to the side, knitting his brows. "I'm not an old fella!"

"I believe you know what I'm saying."

"Yeah, I do," he laughed, shrugging it off. "I'm gonna let yuh get on with your work." He moved away a few steps and then pivoted around. "Yuh gotta be cool, girl!" he said. "Gotta be cool!"

She stood there until he disappeared at the top of the aisle. She was livid at the thought that he...But she forced it out of her mind. He was good-looking, that was all. Not mean, no. Just out for a good time. Oh hell! she thought. Hell!

She went to bingo that evening and won sixty dollars and, coming home, tried convincing herself that good luck was returning. She had to be optimistic and knew it if there was ever to be happiness.

One morning, standing in the bathroom, Nathan felt like going back to bed and crawling in where it was warm. But it wouldn't do. Who would unlock the doors and receive the early deliveries?. He washed and shaved, knowing that a good close shave made him look younger and actually feel better as well. As he slowly slid the razor over his sudsy white face, he smiled at the titillating thought that tonight might be the night. It would be his first time with anyone 'like that'.

After a bagel with butter and a cup of coffee, he left the house. His parents were up, he'd heard them moving around, and so was his brother James. They'd be along shortly, out into the abhorrent cold like himself.

Approaching Food Dreams, his eyes were drawn to the sign. It was old, in dire need of replacement, made out of heavy plastic, with red letters on a white background. He would try and discourage his father from getting it repaired—again. It was just too far gone, dingy-looking, flakes of red missing from the letters; there were even a couple of holes from rocks that had been thrown at it. He saw the tractor trailer waiting in the bay—the dairy order—and he parked quickly and got out of the car. It was cold but not as bad as it had been. He hated winter, cursing it as he jogged across the bleak lot, his shoes crunching in the sand and salt. He shivered, telling himself he just wasn't meant to live in the north. He was part black on his mother's side, his ancestors having come from the West Indies, so he was of the assumption he was genetically predisposed to warmer weather. Perhaps he'd eventually move somehwere where there was no cold.

The day went by without a hitch. Nothing seemed wrong even when it was. He had something to look forward to—and *something* it was! It didn't bother him to have to go out in the cold with no coat to boost a customer's battery. His mind was on other things. Sweeping up broken glass from a jar that had smashed on the floor spilling pickles and splashing juice everywhere was a piece of cake. Even when only half of the bread order arrived he joked about it with the driver, telling him it didn't matter and how would you like a beef wrap out of the deli for lunch? The best of all was when the cashier told him a man had just simply walked away without paying. Nathan shrugged indifferently and thensauntered out the door with a smile to watch the culprit lumbering off with the bulging grocery bags, so heavy they were practically scraping along the sidewalk.

Agatha still spoke to him but merely as a coworker and nothing more. She just didn't want 'that kind' of relationship. She felt used, and, if it went on, Tamara was going to find out sooner or later. He came around in the afternoon, just before the coffee break, and he seemed in good spirits, almost to the point of elation. She spoke to him briefly, focussing on store business.

He maintained a wry smile throughout as if he were nurturing a secret or had a nasty thing to tell.

"Hey, it's busier than I thought it'd be for a Tuesday," he said. "A lot o' shit's gone wrong tuhday, you betcha. It's like the place's cursed. It don't matter though. Things are gain' good for me. I can deal with all o' this when things are goin' good in my life."

"Well, I feel the same," she poked back, hardly looking at him. She was rebunching green onions. "My luck's been better lately."

"Good for you."

She said nothing more and he took the hint, leaving after a pregnant pause. From lowered eyes she caught him leering back at her as he swaggered away. All he had to offer a girl, she thought, was his body.

She was going to go to the casino. She'd been having some luck there lately, having won a couple of hundred dollars a few days ago playing nickel slots. So, after coffee break, she checked with her charm bracelet. The ace of hearts was staring right up at her.

What was it? she wondered, slowly padding back to produce, that made a person's luck change either way? No one knew. Lately hers had been all good and not just financial either. She was free of Nathan and had rejuvenated her pride which was a boost to her ego. Winter was getting on. In a few weeks it would be March and there would be a big thaw and she would see the odd robin hopping around on a patch of grass where the snow had begun to peel away. And then in April bright-eyed daffodils and narcissus would pop out of the ground, eternal harbingers of better days.

Tamara seemed to be a different person, especially in the last little while. Her pregnancy was going well. She was attentive to it, doing what was necessary, seeing her doctor faithfully.

Agatha was glad she was responsible, maintaining healthy habits, going for medical checkups and so forth. She was mostly in good humor too, nothing fazing her or pulling her down. She was generally quite upbeat about life. Perhaps, Agatha thought, it was because she was no longer an object of curiosity at school. The novelty of a pregnant girl, gawking at her and talking about her, had worn off. She was Tamara again, just Tamara—not a freak.

Agatha thought it incredible that their situation had improved to such an extent. It reminded her of the adage, 'What a difference a day makes'.

Nathan put on his better clothes and an extra bit of cologne. His black corduroy pants, heavy and warm, were well-pressed and went strikingly well with his white long-sleeve crew neck. He seldom wore the pants, or even the shiny black boots with their square toes. For a bit of sparkle there was a diamond stud in his ear and a silver chain on his wrist. He'd even had the car washed and, as he walked out to it there in the wide long driveway in the golden glow of the street light, he took considerable pride in its shine.

He started the car, backed out the driveway, and drove slowly away down the well-kept street, where in summer the lawns were green and close-cropped like lovely new carpets. He picked her up at the bus stop in front of the library where she was waiting in a smudgy plexiglas shelter. The shelter was hung with advertising placards and reeked of stale cigarette smoke, the concrete floor was littered with cigarette butts and matches, and Tamara was glad when the little car came round the corner. She was cold and not just a little afraid. Nathan thought she looked smart in her black coat. Her hair was superb too, only a bit tousled from the wind but long, black, and shiny, the way he liked it.

"Yuh bin here long?" he wanted to know, ripping away from the curb.

"No," she told him, holding her little black purse. What was going to happen? she wondered. Where was she going with this man, who was so much older than herself? She'd told him she was eighteen but it was a lie. "My mom was sure inquisitive. She wanted to know where I *was* going in the cold by myself. I told her the library. I don't want to think she might come around and check."

"What's tuh worry, girl? Just hang loose....What'd yuh mean by 'inquisitive'?"

"Nosy," she said. "Wanting to know all your business."

Soon they were speeding down the highway. Nathan kept talking and right now Tamara appreciated it. He mentioned his job, what he did and so on, what he liked and didn't. Some of his plans too, like maybe going back to school to get a diploma. He told her he hadn't finished high school and she was astonished, not letting on, but only said that it would be a good idea. He told her he wanted to get a newer car, something German, because he said they were better made and lasted longer. She didn't know and told him so. And he cursed the weather and she agreed with him that it was a good idea to move away where it was warm, but she wouldn't because of her mom. It occurred to her to ask him what he would do for a living in this new warmer place.

"I can find somethin'," he said, "and hang out at night. Have a good time 'n all."

She wasn't a beach person, she confessed, preferring the shade and cool drinks in the summer. He laughed and said he kind of knew she was a house girl. She admitted that she liked her books and her things nearby—the quiet of her room.

Tamara felt much better than she had at first. She was warming up to him. He didn't seem to be a loud braggart but more reserved and pleasant. He was quite good-looking too, much better than Ethan, who'd been generally uptight.

It was a small club not far from the canal where big steamboats moved by in warmer weather and people watched from the patio. But the canal was closed now and the little bar, called Lock Two, was more or less deserted. Nathan liked it because of its limited popularity and its seclusion. He parked in the lot at the side and was every bit the gentleman, opening the door for Tamara and taking her hand as they made their way past the cars to the entrance. The *last* time he'd been here, he remembered, was with Ella, Tamara's friend. He liked Ella enough because she was good in bed, a rather lush, auburn-haired beauty with big blue eyes who'd confessed to him that she loved sex.

The place was darkish, and bold neon signs advertised different kinds of beer. Tamara thought it was seedy and definitely not for her. She felt intimidated when she noticed everyone's eyes were on them. She thought she would have turned around and left if she'd been by herself. They sat at a table by the wall and she could detect the smell of old beer. Out of the corner of her eye she took a tally of the few customers. They were mostly dressed in old jeans and work clothes.

She ordered an Amaretto and cream which seemed to surprise the bleach-blond waitress. "How 'bout you, Nathan?'

Tamara's eyes opened as wide as saucers. So he'd been here before, had he? And often enough that they remembered his name!

"Draft. Large."

"Blue?"

"Yup.

The waitress left and Tamara gawked at Nathan quizzically.

"What d'yuh think?" he wanted to know.

"About…?"

"This." And he made a wide-sweeping gesture with his hand.

"It's okay," she lied, "not terrible or anything like that."

"Terrible?…It's not that for sure! I just wanted to take ya somewhere where it was quiet." "It's okay, honest. Just for a drink. It's fine. I can stand it."

"Stand it?"

"It's fine, Nathan. Honest!" She reached across the worn old wood table for his hand. "Just one drink. It's fine."

They were holding hands when the drinks came and Nathan took it as a good omen. He had a soft spot for Tamara. She was young and she was beautiful and he was proud to be with her.

"Tab?"

"You betcha," he told the waitress.

He wanted to know about Ethan, whether or not she was going to see him anymore.

Tamara wagged her head, swallowing some of the cool and creamy Amaretto, which tasted delicious. She was sorry she could only allow herself the one. "I'm never going out with him again! I can hardly stand the thought of him. Any guy who's going to be a dad and takes off on his child is a no-good so and so!"

"Whew! I can see yuh got plenty o' spirit, girl! You're burnt over 'im….Hey, I agree yuh can't just do your own thing when yuh got a kid on the way. I know a lot o' guys ramble and leave the girl tuh fight for herself. It ain't right."

She chuckled at the way he put things. He seemed like a big lovable teddy bear—minus the fur. His head, so close-shaven, gleamed even in the dusky bar. Thirty-two, she told herself. He's fourteen years older. Mom would have a fit!

"I didn't know you wore a stud in your ear," she said. "It glitters when you move your head." She was impressed with his clothes and told him he looked nice.

He returned the compliment. “I don’t wear nothin’ like this tuh the store,” he told her. “It’d be a mess in no time ‘n my father sure don’t like men wearin’ earrings either!”

“So…you don’t have a girlfriend? With all the girls that work in the store it’s sure hard to believe.”

“I don’t mess with the staff,” he said. “My father don’t want that neither.”

“Lots of rules.”

“You ain’t kiddin’, girl. Can you believe my father always asks where I’m goin”n how long I’ll be?”

“My mom’s like that.”

“Get your own place.”

“Costs too much. Can’t save no money. It’s the only good thing ‘bout livin’ with your mother ‘n father: you cin save a little dough.”

They drank and watched the goings-on. An older couple left and then three young men in motorcycle jackets came barging in boisterously, charging up to the bar like they owned it. One leered across at Tamara and smiled but she turned her head, ignoring him.

Nathan said, “He’s got an eye for yuh!”

“I don’t have one for him though,” she laughed.

Nathan knew it was time to make his move. She’d told him she didn’t want to be out late, it was a school night, and she didn’t want her mother worrying; that the library was only open till nine, after all, and she might be able to make a story of it somehow until eleven but hardly any later. But, he told her, there were twenty-four hour coffee shops, weren’t there? And wouldn’t that do?

Tamara nursed her Amaretto, savoring its exquisite taste. The cream helped make it delectable and it rolled over her tongue smoothly. She was thinking about having another, not only because of its taste but to prolong the evening. She definitely liked Nathan, despite his lack of refinement. He was 'sweet' as she saw it. She wondered if her feelings for him were out of a need to reaffirm herself and her worthfulness. She supposed there was some truth in it. Tonight, for the first time in a while, she felt wanted by someone other than her mother and her friend Ella. She was in awe of his age too: thirty-two. A grownup! Which made her feel so much more mature, a woman instead of a girl.

When the time came she said, "I'll have another," tapping her cocktail glass with the painted nail of her finger. "It was just so-so good!"

"Hey, let's go for it!"

They had their drinks amid steady chatter from the bar. Three or four people had gone, the quieter ones, but a couple who Tamara thought were about her mother's age couldn't seem to stop giggling, the woman especially, and they were getting on her nerves. The man seemed to be less of a talker. He probably would have been content to just sit there and stare at the wall while he nursed his beer but out of a sense of politeness and respect he pitched in and added to the cacophony too. It was irritating.

"Hey, I know yuh gotta go," Nathan said a bit later.

She'd been gazing at the line of little blue lights on the other side of the canal. They were guide lights for navigation at night. They reminded her of the stars in the sky. She imagined it would be quite nice sitting outside on the patio on a summer night. Quite the romantic thing.

"I don't really want to go," she said, gazing at him with her feline eyes.

"We can go somewhere else," he suggested.

"Like…?"

"Well…" He was hesitant and couldn't quite spell it out.

She knew what it was he had in mind. It was amazing that she felt the same. Everything was happening so fast. She didn't want to go home, at least not yet. Not back to her room again, all alone. She was feeling good too and it would be a shame to put an end to it. He would be only the second one.

Before she knew it they were in a motel room, standing in the dark, kissing each other with a sense of desperation and urgency. She shivered in the coolness and out of a sense of what was about to happen. He was gentle with her, taking his time and, soon enough, she was more settled down and became aroused. She tried to forget everything, everything outside the door. She wanted to enjoy this time with him tonight before it was gone. He was nice, very nice, and she melted in his arms,

Of course he told her all she wanted to hear, actually meaning it, spurred on in the heat of the moment. He stressed her beauty and his appreciation for what she was giving him. He would take care of her too, yes, he wasn't like the other guy, whatever his name was, and it was the beginning of better things certainly. She had nothing to worry about. He was a grownup after all, was he not? And grownups, he stressed, had to be models of repsonsibility. It sounded wonderful, like music in her ears.

Chapter Eight

He was in the cramped office stressing to his father the unworthiness of stocking cumbersome, bard-to-make-money-on three-liter cans of olive oil when Ella phoned him. She was the last thing he needed on a day that had not gone well.

"What," Nathan wanted to know, "do *you* want?"

She asked what he'd been doing and why hadn't he called? He had to admit he'd fantasized about having sex with her again but that was before he'd been out with Tamara.

"It's over," he told her point blank. His father, a large, bald man, was sitting there shaking his head. "I ain't gonna be seek'" yuh no more, girl."

She wanted to know what had happened and he argued with her for a couple of minutes back and forth like a ping-pong ball. Then he slapped the receiver down in a huff. The bitch just wouldn't take no for an answer.

He looked at his father and broke into that broad smile of his. "People ain't buyin"em," he drilled on, making abrupt, slicing gestures with his hand for emphasis. "They're too goddam big and they bin tellin' me they're tough tub open....There ain't no profit in 'em, dad. They're sellin' olive oil all over for a bit over cost. Tuh hell with the cans, I say! We only sold two the whole week."

His father sat back in the chair and clasped his hands behind his head. "You win," he said. "No more three-liter olive oil it is."

Nathan went to the dairy cooler and, clipboard in hand, began poring over everything. He had to make up an order but his mind was on Tamara. She was a darling, he mused, a real good looker, as sweet as pie. He was smitten. He had the feeling that this would be something more, something very special. Perhaps it was her vulnerability that drew him to her. After all she was going to have a baby and he felt sorry for her, for her situation. That guy she'd been going out with, he'd done a bad thing

leaving her in the lurch. And his own kid too! Ironically, he realized that from that misfortune had come his good luck. They'd met and now here they were, going out again tomorrow night. Just thinking about sex with her drove him wild, a young, pregnant, dark- haired beauty. He'd asked her if she was going back to Ethan and her answer was a firm, decisive "No!"

Carol spent her days off catching up on things she didn't have time to do otherwise. It was a Saturday afternoon and she had a rare whole weekend away from the busy little coffee shop where she served at the drive-thru window. As she poked the vacuum beneath the coffee table she could feel perspiration breaking out on her forehead. She flipped the machine off, removed her sweatshirt and tossed it on a chair, then took a deep breath and sighed. She knew it would be good to lose a few pounds and maybe even get rid of some of her red curly hair, cut it short for coolness and a new look. But she was going to wait till spring for that. She surveyed what she could see of the apartment from her vantage point there in the living-room. It was too big a place for one person, much too much work, and things were getting pretty shabby. The rent was not cheap either. She was going to look for a newer, brighter place, smaller, with less rent to pay. She went over to the window and peered out. There wasn't much snow on the ground and it had been a fairly good winter so far, not too cold except for a few days, and that had made it a lot easier to walk down to the end of the street to work. She watched a car go by in the hazy sunlight. It was a quiet enough street, there was that. All of Awappich was quiet, not much ever happening other than an occasional fire or a drowning in the fast-moving creek. Perhaps it was the tedium that had driven her to do what she did. Grant was a good-looking hunk, there weren't many around like him. She felt a pathetic, mournful tug inside. That had been the best time of her life, the affair with Grant, and she didn't regret it for a moment. She believed she'd been in love with him. He'd been hers really not Agatha's and that obsessive thought had been boring a hole in her ever since his death. She'd considered calling his wife before a few times but had never gotten up the nerve. They knew each other, though she didn't think Agatha would recognize her voice after so long. Her mind began churning. The temptation was there to get it off her chest, to be victorious at least in one thing in her life. It would help to alleviate the pain and trivialize the other failures, the disappointments—things that had not gone right.

With a cigarette in her trembling hand, she poked out the numbers and held the receiver tight to her ear. The phone was ringing and then a woman answered.

"Grant was mine!" was all she said.

She was shaking and collapsed into a chair, holding her head in her hands. She'd done it anyhow, she'd gotten up the courage to earn her victory. She knew the nervousness would pass and then there would be elation. At long last!

Agatha was sitting on the sofa toying with the bright blue peacock feathers. She had an idea who it had been but couldn't be sure. The voice was somewhat familiar. Three words only, swift and to the target, like an arrow. She'd tried to get the number back with the phone feature, but the caller ID had been blocked. She'd been on her way out to get a few things at the store when the phone rang and was sitting there now with her coat on all bundled up with a toque on her head. It looked warm outside because of the dull sunlight but it was deceptive. If it had been Carol, she thought, why now? Why had she waited so long? And why had she bothered at all? Weren't some things best left unsaid? But maybe it hadn't been her, it could have been someone else. But she doubted it. She'd had her suspicions about Grant from time to time, that was about all, and she'd just swept them under the rug. There were so many other things to deal with now, she couldn't let herself be taken up by anything ancient.

When she got back from the corner store Tamara was in the kitchen having a toasted egg sandwich and a large glass of milk.

"I bought more," Agatha said, hoisting two half-gallons onto the counter. "When are you going?"

"In a half hour."

"Not too short."

"I know, mom. You keep telling me that."

"You look good with long hair."

"Who called? I thought I heard the phone ring."

Tamara's eyes were so much like her father's, thought Agatha, dark, wonderful gems. "I don't know, dear," she mumbled, and turned round to put the milk away.

"I don't understand."

Her daughter wasn't going to let it go.

"There was no one on the line, dear….0h, I just remembered, they're coming to get the car."

It was after five when the tow truck hauled the jalopy away. Agatha and Tamara watched at the window. It seemed to Agatha like the end of an era, the car a symbol of her defunct marriage. They'd given her fifty dollars for it which she could use. If it hadn't been for the landlord bugging her to get rid of it ("The goddam rust bucket's gotta go."), she probably would have left the thing there forever. Out the snowswept lot it went in the fading light, like a fish caught on a line, past its quiet parked siblings out onto the road, quickly disappearing. Tears stood in her eyes while Tamara cried.

Agatha left early for bingo, sparing Tamara the need to go and hide somewhere where Nathan could pick her up. They went for Chinese food right in town, to a dismal little place that was poorly lit and chilly too.

"I best let you do the orderin'," Nathan advised, and then said, "I wanted tuh take yuh to a real nice place, Tam. Yuh sure it's okay?"

"Yes. Absolutely! Wait until you taste the food!"

They were sitting by the wall and a red candle on the table kept flickering, casting eery jumping shadows, making for a Halloweenish atmosphere. It was busy, and bubbling bits of conversation percolated all around.

"The smells are making me hungry," Tamara said, folding her hands on the table.

"I shoulda taken yuh tuh the Italian place. It's all decorated up real nice. Nice surrotmdin's 'n all. Yuh know, every Chinese place I ever bin in has the same pictures on the walls. Gardens, and people in those white 'n red silk things and those there… what d'ya call 'em?"

"Pagodas."

"Yup."

"The food is what counts."

The waitress was Chinese, milky pale, in a tight body-fitting dress with a motif of pink cyclamens. She welcomed them with a smile, set down the menus, and took their drink orders. "Take your time," she said. "Enjoy, yes."

When she'd gone Nathan said it looked like she was wearing a sock.

Tamara told him she had a similar dress but minus the flowers. "But I sure can't wear it anymore."

Nathan smiled, but he took the pregnancy seriously. There were grave complications for him and every time he heard the word he winced. It would have been so much easier if she'd *not* been. Look how beautiful she is! he marvelled. Instead of poring over the menu, his eyes were on her. She'd had her hair cut, or so it seemed, but it was almost as long, shiny and black even in the dull light. Her head, lowered now, conferred a spiritual, almost heavenly look on her face.

"D'you see anything you want, Nathan?...What are you looking at?"

"You," he said, glowing brightly, revealing his nice white teeth.

Heck, she marvelled, he's so good-looking I can hardly stand it! He'd overdressed, it seemed, probably for her. He wore a charcoal blazer over a fiery red shirt and he made for a terrific snapshot. No matter what he had on he wasn't hard to look at. His eyes were irresisitible, almond-shaped, kind and brimming with good humor.

She had a small glass of tomato juice with a crescent of lemon while he took a glass of red house wine. She did the ordering and he sat there looking on, his eyes flickering from the China doll jotting it all down to the beauty across from him. His girlfriend, as he was coming to think of Tamara, had a definite touch of class and elegance. The food was very good, just as Tamara had said it would be, and hot too which Nathan appreciated. It seemed fresh, to have been just made, and not heated up in a microwave or otherwise.

"I told you," Tamara said, eating with gusto. She'd put on weight, how much she didn't know, purposely avoiding the scale. It was definitely off limits. This kind of thing, dining out, was a real treat, and she was going to indulge. It was mostly a lot of vegetables, she rationalized, and you could eat and eat.

"This is good stuff, Tam! You betcha!"

Nathan was enjoying himself and Tamara was glad. She took a vicarious pleasure in trying to satisfy him. Though she'd not known him for long she had a strong sense that he might be *the* one in spite of his age. But then, after Ethan, after what he'd done, well…who could say? A positive thing was that Nathan was taking quite an interest in the baby.

The movie was about the California gold rush and Nathan loved it because it concerned a family business. The company not only assayed the miners' gold but coined it too and made ingots so it could more easily be used as legal tender. There was a love story and it appealed to Tamara because the young woman was about her own age. She met a young man who'd come west from Pennsylvania

seeking his fortune in the gold fields but who was not having any luck. She fell in love with him but her mother and father disapproved, painting a bleak picture of the future for the couple.

"Nathan, Nathan…"

"What?"

Tamara told him she needed to go to the ladies room. She quietly slipped down the row of seats and pattered quickly up to the exit between tiers of ghostly faces peering out of the darkness. She suddenly did not feel well and thought it might be something she'd eaten but when she realized there was a strange stickiness between her legs she cringed with fear. In the washroom, alone in the bright light, with the sound of the movie throbbing through the wall, she saw a stark picture of horror when she rose to flush the toilet. The water was full of blood.

Agatha *was* holding the horseshoe and gazing at the two big cardboard boxes heaped full of Grant's things. They were going to go to the Salvation Army; a truck would be coming around Monday and could she please leave them in the hallway? Rubbing the horseshoe between her fingers, she realized how little she cared for Grant. She hardly felt sad and was glad to see the end of his personal things, a final and, she had to admit, a fond farewell.

She went and sat on the sofa and looked at the horseshoe. It was silver, and a man had given it to her at a carnival when she was a little girl. She'd been around a ring a couple of times on the back of a pony and it was her prize for being good .

The phone rang, jarring her.

It was Nathan. He was upset, his voice panicky. "Aggy, Aggy! Come lull the hospital! It's Tamara."

Part Two

Chapter One

The apartment was up to North American standards in every way and Olivia was delighted. She really hadn't expected anything so new or well-appointed. There was even a microwave in the small kitchen. The building itself, she guessed, couldn't have been more than a few years old, all in white with a courtyard and a fountain and a garden full of tropical plants and flowers. It was close to the beach as well and that first night she lay in bed listening to the waves as they broke along the shore. Her body was tired but her mind was wide awake and, in the all pervasive darkness, she felt a stab of fear. Here she was, she realized, all alone in a strange but certainly beautiful part of the world—and with no one to count on but herself. She'd done it though, she'd made it! And she congratulated herself on that, certain she would survive too. She was elated to have now what she really hadn't bad before—independence, freedom—and she told herself she was going to get along and get along well. She recalled bits and pieces of her former life with mixed feelings. There'd been good and bad.

She'd been living in Bridle Path in a luxurious seven-bedroom mansion that resembled a castle. It was made of sand-colored brick that glowed at night in the wash of floodlights.

The grounds were well-kept, vast enough even for a short ride on horseback, the lawns soft and green in the summer when numerous flower beds came to life in a panoply of color among the small stands of shrubs and trees. The mansion came complete with battlements and turrets., even a moat with a functioning drawbridge. The moat was stocked with goldfish and on bright sunny days she gazed down dreamily from high above and watched them sparkling like gold flecks caught in a breeze. She had plenty of time to let her mind wander. She didn't work. Marius wanted it that way and in better weather she'd stroll down the flagstone path to a Victorian bench to read in the shade of a red maple. She was surprised at how laid back she'd become. She didn't like to use the word 'lazy' but it lurked in her mind. Everything was taken care of, wasn't it? Or so her reasoning went. The cooking, the cleaning, the care of the grounds and the automobiles, even the laundry. Why should she do anything other than indulge herself when she didn't have to?

She remembered pausing at the mirror there at the top of the staircase, a large thing like a picture window with a heavy ornate gilt frame, and seeing just how awful she looked. Why, she'd taken on years before her time! She peered closer, into her almond-shaped eyes, and saw how unsettled and glazed with concern they were. Nonetheless she could still detect tiny sequins of hope. She stepped back and smiled and saw the prettiness underneath all the turmoil. Her hair could be fixed up easily enough, perhaps with a few blond streaks and highlighting, and she was only too aware of what a little makeup could do—bolder eyelashes, a touch of eye shadow, some coloring on her cheeks. Her high cheekbones came from her grandmother and her prim little mouth needed only lipstick, nothing loud, something subtle as a whisper. She stepped back and saw that her figure was still adolescent for thirty-three. What made Marius flirt with other women? she wondered. Why did he do what he did?Perhaps if she hadn't seen him in that doorway with her at New Year's his absences from home wouldn't seem so ominous and her dinners alone would be more acceptable. Even his arriving in the wee hours, though loathed, might be tolerated. He was a lawyer after all and a well-known one at that, and there should be some leeway. Deep down however she knews things had gone too far.

The sun-drenched study had become a refuge for her, a place away from the real world. It was just the thing with its warmth and brightness from the cathedral window that let in the afternoon sun through sheer white curtains that cascaded to the gleaming hardwood floor like the folds of an angel's gown. She kept all her books here, her friends as she called them, in tall oak cases, and her coin collection too.

She'd taken out the album of Canadian small cents and sat at the quaint little Edwardian desk with its drop leaf and its pigeon holes and sipped her tea in a state of 'oubli'. Coin collecting had become a wonderful escape. She loved art and went to all the big shows, and she saw coins as art too. She liked the way they took on patina over time in colors of the rainbow. She opened the album and smiled. The one-cent coins were all red and lustrous, just like new—'uncirculated' was the term—and they were lined up in neat horizontal rows up and down each page. They were beautiful to look at and they made her feel good. She had the idea that maybe she could start a business buying and selling coins. Heavens, wouldn't that be swell! She remembered the coin Marius had brought home some time ago, a piece involved in litigation over a dispute regarding hereditary rights. It was a proof example of an 1875-H Canadian ten-cent piece that had not a mark on it, with perfect mirror fields and a portrait of Queen Victoria that was as white as snow.

"It is worth a small fortune," she could still hear Marius saying in his deep confident voice, "and I stand to make plenty of money if I can finagle things my way."

What a rogue he was, she mused. Money was his god and he cared little about other people.

From that time on, from the beauty she'd see in that one coin, she became a coin collector. Marius thought she was going crazy. She began travelling to coin shows, even flew to the United States and Europe to attend them, and once to Brazil. She loved Brazil. *It* was the place for her!

She'd heard the wind whistling and when she turned her head she was startled by the snow flakes firing up against the window like little demons. She hated winter. As she stared at the flakes she wondered if she'd ever go back to work in a library. She didn't think so and she didn't mind either. She'd done it for a while and then it had become just a job, quitting fmally at Marius' repetitive urging.

Her husband was home on time that day but short on words. She could tell it had been a hard go and the pins hadn't quite fallen the way he would have liked. As he sat sullenly hunched over the long dinner table like a big defeated football player, she figured he must be contemplating all the 'if onlies' and telling himself he'd just have to do better tomorrow. How had he missed this and how had he missed that? Why the one thing and not the other? He'd told her more than once that law was complicated but could be manipulated and that, with a little more experience, he'd never have anything less than a perfect day. Wrapped up within himself like the inside of a golf ball, he ate his roast beef dinner, oblivious of his surroundings, especially of her. He was thihy-five, husky, with thick broad shoulders and an intimidating look on his ruddy face. He ate with his elbows on the table and his forearms cocked like a fighter up by his face, with a fork in one hand and a knife in the other. He cut his food aggressively and brought it to his mouth with a grudge. He saw it as him against the wily forces of life. His name was Marius Lane and didn't they all know that?

Finally he'd said something, but with a slice of sarcasm: "So, Olive, how many books did you get through today?" His wide flat thumb with its crude flaking nail kept working hard at the fork as he spoke, up and down on the handle it went as if trying to rub something away. "Or did you scoot downtown in your convertible that kind Marius bought for you and waste some more of his money on another coin?" There was silence and his piercing blue eyes became steely as drill bits. "Well? Well?" He began to shout. "Speak up, will you? Speak up! I can't hear you!"

The housekeeper, Theodosia, a young plump Greek woman with hair as black as ink, was just about to step into the dining room with a tureen of gravy but had retreated back into the sanctuary of the kitchen.

"I did what I always do, you see," Olivia recalled telling him in a quavering voice. "I did what you want me to do: I stayed home, yes. You can't expect me to just sit in a chair and look at the four walls."

She'd been surprised at the forcefulness of her words. This was a new way of dealing with him. Her self-confidence had been crumbling like an old wall but there were indications it was making a comeback. Marius said no more and went on eating. She couldn't tell at all what he might be thinking. He glowered at her with his hot eyes every now and again and then left the room when he was done. Most likely, she thought, he's gone to his den to play war with his lead soldiers and his toy tanks and airplanes. "I go to war every day," he liked to tell her, referring to his profession. He was a war freak, interested in anything that had to do with it.

Theodosia had brought in some tea and cleared the table, while she lingered over a dish of petits fours. She'd taken one and nibbled on it, wondering if she could get up enough courage. She listened to the tick-tock of the grandfather clock in the next room. She felt no one could go on like this.

When her passport came she was thrilled to think she'd taken the first step. She was sitting beside a floor lamp in her study in a wing chair. She opened the passport and giggled girlishly at the photo. A real mug shot! So serious! Why, she looked forty or more! Maybe it was her hair, she thought, just plain and hanging like icicles or her face pleading for makeup.

Time wore on and her instinct to survive had pushed her to take the next steps. There was the phone call to the airline, vaccinations, and the choice of clothing.

Early in April she'd packed her car and driven away. Her heart was pounding. The warmth was unusual for the time of year. Stopping at the end of the driveway, she put on her sunglasses and lowered the window halfway to let in the spring air. She saw small leaves on the beech trees across the way and grass that was so green it looked like it was lit up. She turned around and looked at the castle. She prayed never to return. And now here she was. She closed her eyes and after a long while, with the hushed sound of the waves in her ears and thoughts of an exciting new life, she fell asleep.

The next morning she dressed in old shorts and a T-shirt and went down the steps to the office in bare feet to see if she could get some coffee and toast. It was lovely and very warm already with the sun just tucked in behind a fluffly white cloud and she could smell the mild tang of the salt in the air and the lush, earthy greenness of all the things that were growing close by. She smiled amiably at a couple of young men who were cleaning up the garden, picking up twigs and older foliage, and saw with considerable surprise that they were identical twins, each with swarthy skin and dark hair and dressed in khaki shirts and pants. They also bore a striking resemblance to Adinaldo, the landlord. They stopped what they were doing when they saw her and watched with intense curiosity as she timidly made her way over to the office.

Olivia opened the door and stepped inside. A clock on the wall said it was ten minutes after ten. She hadn't slept so late in years! A woman came through a doorway and asked if she could be of any help. She was wearing a cotton floral print dress in green and had long black hair pinned back on each side with sequin white berets.

"I don't have any food upstairs," Olivia explained. "I'm just new here, you see, and I was wondering if I could perhaps buy a cup of coffee and some toast."

"For you for free," the woman smiled. "You wait. I get for you, yes?"

"That would be swell."

She sat in a leather chair and waited, arms folded, gazing up at the pictures on the wall. They were neat drawings in ink of beach scenes, likely inspired by the immediate area. The pictures were in thin black frames and the glass, like everything else in the office, was shiny and spotless.

She took her coffee and toast back upstairs on a little plastic tray, noting gratefully the two dollops of jam. The twins in the garden were watching her and when they saw her looking they gave her a wave and a timid smile.

She was hungry and ate the toast with gusto, spooning up all the jam, then sat out on the terrace overlooking the tropical garden while she sipped her coffee and observed the twins. At present they were working on trimming a cashew tree that was growing a little awkwardly, much thicker on the one side than the other, obviously hoping for some symmetry. The whole garden was like that, she remarked, everything well-placed and neat, very straight up, with hardly any overgrowth at all, almost as if the plants and the flowers and the trees were not real but had been made by hand and brought in and set about just right. The perfect setting reminded her of Adinaldo, the man with the deep-set dark eyes who'd picked her up at the airport. He *was* the owner's son, she'd found out, and he'd struck her as someone who was probably too critical and would demand perfection. Why, as soon as she'd gotten out of the car he'd taken a handkerchief and wiped down the handles of the doors!

She slouched down in the rattan chair, stretching her pale legs. She told herself with delight she was going to have to work on her suntan. She could hear the waves collapsing along the shore more loudly than last night. Screeching cantankerously, a trio of what she took to be parrots swiftly flew by overhead behind the swaying branches of a tall palm tree.She wondered if Adinaldo would mind her getting a parrot of her own. She could buy a large cage and keep it in her little apartment and have a friend to talk to and on nicer days such as this she could bring the bird outside.

In a while, about to doze off with the soft caress of the sea breeze on her face, she opened her dreamy amber eyes to the sound of pebbles crunching. She peered down and saw Adinaldo getting out of the Mercedes. He wasted no time and marched purposefully toward the office.

In a few minutes she went down to see him. She wanted to take care of some business and ask him a few questions, and a very special favor too. He was standing behind the counter, wearing fashionable eyeglasses with caramel-colored frames and studying a ledger.

"Yes?" he said, with a hint of irritation.

"I want to give you some money," she told him. "It seems very nice here. I'll be staying on." "Your rent is paid until the end of the month. We'll leave things until then."

"If you wish." She watched him lower his eyes to the ledger. "May I ask you a favor, Mr. Hildegard? I'm sorry to be a bother, this is very important."

Adinaldo took off his glasses and set them down. "Go ahead."

"I would prefer that no one know I am here. It is the only favor I ask."

"Your wish is granted," Adinaldo said. "Is there anything else, Mrs. Lane?"

"Can you tell me if there are any coin stores in the city?"

"For collectors?"

"Yes."

Adinaldo gazed at something outside, his mysterious eyes far away and unsettled. For a moment he said nothing. Then curtly, "I do not know."

He put his glasses back on and turned and disappeared through the doorway.

Olivia spent the rest of the day getting her apartment in order and then took a crowded bus into Fortaleza to do some banking, put her coins in a safe deposit box, and do some grocery shopping. Almost everyone in business in the colorful, crowded, bustling city, spoke English and she had no trouble getting things done. As soon as she left the bank with her wad of reals, she scooted off to the grocery store and bought enough to fill four big bags, which she had trouble getting back to the apartment more because of their awkwardness than their weight. When she got off the bus she was sweating and grimy. An old man in a straw hat who got off with her helped her carry the bags across the street and right up to her front door. She gave him a real for his effort and his sun-baked and weatherbeaten face beamed with joy.

By the time it was all over with and the groceries and things put away, the afternoon was all but gone and she was feeling the pangs of hunger. She fell into a chair and just sat there gathering her thoughts. It seemed to her that not many of the apartments were rented out, as evidenced by the number of cars. She realized it was off-season. She hadn't had much chance to be lonely because she'd been chasing after necessities. But now, in the quiet of the moment, with the chores done, loneliness settled over her like a dark cloak. It was a terrible feeling and she gripped the arms of the chair as if they were buoys of safety in a rough sea. The sun, too, was acting the part, sinking quickly, and the shadows were lengthening, soon to disappear and blend into the landscape like the final spirits of the day. Everyone, she thought gloomily, was a stranger. The buildings were strange and unfamiliar too, as was the vegetation, so were the streets, the sky, the sounds—and this apartment she wanted to adopt as her new home. There were no pictures on the walls and the furniture, though nice enough and comfortable—why, it seemed alien too! Glancing around, she decided to get some simple pretty pictures and a few small plants. And a parrot; but she'd have to wait and see on that. Perhaps fussy Mr. Hildegard wouldn't allow it. She guessed he'd tell her it was the screeching and squawking when deep down he'd probably be worrying mostly about the itsy bitsy mess birds made—a few feathers and scattered seed.

That evening she saw Adinaldo drive out of the courtyard around eight. He did the same thing the next evening and the one after that, at the same time. He never came back and his car wasn't there when she woke up in the morning. She figured he lived somewhere else.

Olivia quickly began to adjust to life in Brazil. It was always warm and she liked that, and she liked living by the seaside too. She could just go out anytime and stroll along the beach, dipping her toes in the warm bubbly foam along the shore or splashing right in and letting the warm salt water wash over her like a velvety caress. She began to take on the carefree look of a young native and the brown of her hair began to resemble the color of the sand along the shore. Her face became brown and her brows sandy too and because of the contrast her teeth seemed much whiter. One day while she was wandering among the sand dunes not far from where the sand met the grassland and the scattered high palm trees, she saw a fisherman standing out in the water struggling to keep his balance in the waves and hold on to his fishing pole. It was windy and far out over the inky blue ocean she could see a lovely ridge of clouds in lavender and pink riding high in the wind and it made her feel wonderful all of a sudden, like the world was hers and the future just an open book with terrific possibilities. For a moment she forgot about the phone calls she'd made but when a good gust of wind came up and rattled the punky heads of the palms, the conversations came back to mind. With her amber eyes peeled on the fisherman, she dug on slowly through the sand recalling her mother's words:

"You ought not to have done such a thing. They're all talking and you must come back. Grownup women do not do this. Where is your sense of responsibility? What ever happened to 'until death do you part'? You had a lovely home, Olivia, the very best of everything. You could have worked things out with Marius—you still can. I can't understand what more anyone could want."

A life, mother, she reasoned, my own and, if a husband, one that is dedicated and faithful—oh, and somewhat friendly!

On the other hand, Brenda had been reservedly positive and somewhat encouraging:

"I think you did the right thing, Oily. It was a shock though. For all of us. Marius deserved it. Maybe you should have told him. I think that would have been better. One good thing, you can afford to stay away for a while without worrying where your next meal's coming from. That's a plus. Just hang out for a while, Oily. Have fun. Do your own thing. You don't get to be a kid twice very often."

Yes, she thought, coming up now to where the fisherman was, that was all Brenda: live for today with not a care for tomorrow. A fun girl all in all but a good friend. She was someone real and the only person who'd had misgivings about her marrying Marius. Olivia could feel the warm salty spray of the froth from the waves carried on the wind, spattering in a fine mist across her face. She licked her lips and could taste the salt on her tongue and, stopping there in the sand and turning to watch the fisherman, she had visions of golden brown French fries spattered with vinegar and sprinkled with plenty of salt, and her mouth watered. She thought she could hear the fisherman singing above the steady rush of the waves. She listened closely but couldn't be sure. She retreated back a way and sat in the sand where it was high and dry and watched the fellow as he tried almost desperately to maintain an upright position in the foamy white veins of the eddies before the next wave came along trying to bowl him over. His struggles reminded her of her own. Here he was, and just for a fish, fighting a war of sorts. Given her great goal of achieving independence, she was sure it was worth struggling with lingering feelings of homesickness and loneliness in order to win out. And when she saw the fisherman finally lift a flip-flopping fish out of the water and net it with a show of legerdemain, she clapped and cheered.

The fisherman's name, she learned, was Baldochi.

"Oi, como sao?" Olivia asked him.

"Born!" He smiled and wiped his glistening face with the back of his arm. "Pode ser geladeira. Issa seria melhor."

She understood that he thought it was a little too hot. As for herself, she was feeling quite comfortable. As they walked side by side in the sand, Baldochi carried his old fishing pole in one hand and, in the other, a rusty pail full of water in which two good-sized red snapper, the color of a pretty sunset, kept flip-flopping about in a final quest for freedom. Olivia felt sorry for them but then she knew they wouldn't be wasted. This man, with a shadow of salt and pepper stubble on his suntanned face, would take them home and eat them, probably share them with a wife and perhaps an older child. He spoke some English, albeit not much, but they both succeeded in communicating what was on their minds. When she told Baldochi where she lived he stopped in his tracks and his face, now folded up like the bellows of an accordeon, took on a sudden, very serious expression. She wondered what was wrong and he told her without mincing words, his eyes turning into glaring black beads:

"Mr. Hildegard, he is a mysterious man," he warned in broken English. "I do not believe that you can trust him. He has a secret. And his father too, he has a secret. Everyone believes this but no one knows what this secret is. You must be careful. You are young and Adinaldo, he is young too. You do not want to be in their secret with them."

Chapter Two

The next day it rained hard and, in the morning, not long after Adinaldo had arrived at the beach apartments, Olivia went into the office to ask him that favor that had been on her mind. He smiled at her in a kind way which she found encouraging but he said nothing, instead pulling out from under the counter a roll of what she took at once to be large coins. He plunked them down on the counter. They were neatly done up in manilla paper and she read in ink, marked on the roll, 1922-S $20 gold.

"What is this?" she wanted to know, touching the roll. Adinaldo adjusted his glasses and set both his perfectly manicured hands on the edge

of the counter. "It is a part of my coin collection," he told her, hoping to strike the right chord. "I wanted to show them to you. I have many

other coins too. Gold are my favorite. I like gold. I think it is the feel of it and the weight. And the color too. Like a sun that has been tamed."

Olivia, though a bit perplexed, had to grin at the analogy. "Well put!"

"Go ahead, open it."

Olivia was thinking about the fisherman she'd met on the beach and the secret he said both father and son shared. Was this roll of coins a part of it? Before long, large gold disks were falling against one another like drunks in a lineup. The coins were lustrous. She picked one up to look at it.

"It's a United States twenty-dollar gold piece," Adinaldo said. "A Saint-Gaudens double eagle dated 1922 and with an 'S' mintmark."

"Where did you get them all?" she pressed him, more interested in the story behind their acquisition than in the coins themselves.

"My father purchased them years ago," Adinaldo said. "He bought many as an investment. have to invite you to my house sometime and show you more. We have beautiful paintings as well."

Olivia made no comment but placed the coin she had in her hand back with the rest and asked him about the parrot. Since running into Baldochi, she didn't trust him; there was just something about him she couldn't put her finger on. As soon as he told her she could have a parrot she thanked him and left the office.

The parrot's name was Blaze and he was an Amazon, large and green with splashes of red and yellow on his head, wings, and tail. He was about eight years old. Olivia was happy to have him around and, there in his new big cage by the window that looked out on the courtyard, he soon became accustomed to life with his new owner. Blaze ate well which she knew was a sure sign of contentment. She gave him a shower every four or five days and he seemed to love it, talking afterwards in Portuguese. She had been studying Portuguese on her own now for quite some time and she understood his bird talk to be something along the lines of: "Hello, how are you? Time to eat, huh huh, time to eat"; "What's that? What's that?"; "Not nice, not nice."; "Where you goin', dear? *Where* you goin'?". She made sure Blaze had everything: a lava block to keep his beak in perfect shape, a concrete perche for self manicuring, and plenty of food supplements beyond basic parrot food. mix—bean sprouts and alfalfa, for example; and just about any kind of fruit and vegetable, but never avocado. That, she had been told, was poison to parrots.

The apartment had become her new home and as she sat on the sofa against the wall one rainy afternoon some two months later, she looked around proudly. The place, she told herself, was quite comfortable, very inviting, and she always looked forward to returning whenever she was away. There were some simple prints on the walls in cheap frames, mostly of flowers and birds native to the area. There was one in particular of a covey of egrets leaving land and starting out over a rough sea. The birds reminded her of the day she'd left home—if home it could be called—to come south to Fortaleza and Brazil. She hoped in her imagination that the egrets would find at least as much contentment as she had wherever they were going. She glanced around at the furniture and, though it was mismatched, she thought it was wonderful. There were rattan chairs with pretty-colored cushions and end tables in French colonial, albeit a bit battered but perfectly good and functional. The sofa she was sitting on was done over in a rougher, durable, light green tweed. And the ottoman on which she often rested her feet was in navy blue vinyl, with a short, straight gash in the side. She kept the apartment just about spotless which was no easy task given its proximity to the beach and the sea. The salt air managed to set down a tough grime on everything, especially glass, and she noticed that even some of her newer books, standing nicely in two large bookcases, were beginning to yellow after just short exposure.

From time to time she ran into Baldochi fishing along the shore and she always waited around to speak to him before continuing along through the smooth, sculpted sand dunes down the beach on her regular afternoon walks. One day she made it a point to go the other way, toward a more popular beach and an outdoor patio bar, where a cluster of red and yellow umbrellas seemed to sprout from the sand like giant mushrooms. She bad brought a little money with her to have a drink and she sat at a table close by the water and ordered a South Side Fizz. L000king out to sea, she guessed it would rain later. Threatening deep gray clouds, like boulders, hovered over the dark blue of the ocean where gashes of white, like wounds, cut frothily into the tops of the waves. She watched the gulls circling right there overhead, just a way from the patio umbrellas, squawking pitifully and waiting for any scrap of food to find a way clear.

She paid for her drink in reals, tipping the waitress generously and informing her she'd only be having the one, "Obrigado." She sipped it and the cold sweet and sour gin was refreshing and wet on her tongue and the back of her throat in the rush of warm salty air coming in off the water. The breeze kept ruffling the scalloped edge of the umbrella over her head making it flap from time to time while the umbrella squeaked and groaned in its moorings. She saw that the patio bar was not busy today nor was the beach crowded aither. A few sunworshippers, either sitting up or lying down, waited on their towels for the sun to make a lasting appearance, while a couple of dozen bathers, mostly children, frolicked around in the ocean, laughing and calling out and mostly having a good time despite the cloudiness. On sunny days, Olivia had seen before, people would swarm like bees all over the place. But she liked it just like this, mostly quiet, with only the sound of the sea and the gulls and the sighing wind and, occasionally, bits of conversation from the few customers across the way. She had no shoes on and her toes flirted with the grains of sand that had blown up off the beach onto the makeshift wooden floor. She wore old blue jeans, tattered at the cuffs and torn open in neat long slices at the knees. She had on a red T-shirt and her hair, growing longer, blew about her brown face in a frenzy. She'd never been happier and she'd certainly never go back. Her amber eyes were calm and their

skittishness gone, replaced by a dreamy, velvety look, full of the present, with little or no concern for either the past or the future.

She thought about Adinaldo and chuckled at the idea of ever going out with him. There was no way, it was just never going to happen. For one thing she enjoyed being alone with no obligation to anyone, and she did not trust the man. He was good-looking mough, sure, but something was up with him. She felt Baldochi was right.

As time went by it became increasingly clear to her that she was going to have to move. She had stopped making excuses and finally told Adinaldo she did not want to go out with him. He had taken it hard. And his way of dealing with it was to snub her and generally be unfriendly, not doing her

any favors at all, such as running her into town on a whim or picking things up for her, or fixing a leaky tap or a running toilet. The final straw was when he raised her rent through the roof.

She began to spend more time in Fortaleza, with the thought in mind of maybe buying a viable business there, somewhere downtown, in a nicer part, a boutique maybe with living quarters right above. She realized the impracticality of just buying and selling coins to collectors and besides she had only a few Latin American pieces. Coins could always be an addendum later to what was already there. So she had a cup of tea here and a drink there, frequenting the little cafés and wandering through the shops, getting to know people and gathering information. She'd spend time too scanning the ads in the papers for just the right shop for sale, visiting a few, but mostly they were in depressed areas, older and rundown, and with little promise. Finally she was put on to a little place right near a busy corner by a young man of about thirty who said that his grandmother was getting out of business because his grandfather had died and she no longer could do it all herself.

Olivia wanted the store as soon as she saw it. It was small, appeared very well-kept from the outside, and it was in a busy, somewhat prestigious area. There was a boutique just next door that sold fine leather shoes and, sitting right on the corner, an Internet café with an outdoor patio where you could sit in the shade of a yellow umbrella sipping coffee or cocktails, or spooning up ices in fruit

flavors.

She went into the store excited, acutely aware of her accelerated heartbeat. This would be it, she told herself with assurance, the ultimate breakaway. She saw at once there were a number of people milling about. She admired the old antique cash register. It was manual and rang with a jingle as the drawer slid lazily out. It was made of wood and had brass keys. She shuffled up and down the aisles taking everything in. The obvious specialty was native dinnerware, all of it handmade and hand-painted and with a high price. She thought it was beautiful and could tell at a glance that most, if not all, of the customers were tourists who, she knew, were often indifferent to prices. There were sets of dishes, and cups and saucers that went along, with small cream and sugar carafes, and teapots too. She strolled over to the textiles where blankets and sheets abounded in every imaginable color and size, and there were smaller rugs too, for the kitchen perhaps or the bathroom, or for laying just inside or out a front door.

Not long after the rain began, people stopped coming in and she went over to the wrinlded and careworn older woman and introduced herself. She told her how she'd found out about the place and was the store just for rent or might the whole building be up for sale?

The woman, whose name was Marie, wore a red silk kerchief over her crinkly salt and pepper hair and she gazed up mournfully with narrow grayish eyes and managed a pouty sort of smile. "I am going to sell the building," she said with finality, placing her hands on the counter. "It has come to that. My husband is dead and it is too much for one who is my age. You—you are interested?"

Olivia was surprised to hear not the slightest trace of an accent. "You speak English so very

well."

"I have been here for nearly forty-five years," Marie said, beaming. Her teeth were large and white and very good. "I know that you are a foreigner."

"Canada."

"Do you speak French then?"

"Not well, no."

"My father and mother, they were from France. I lived there in the city of Nimes until I was twenty nine."

Thereafter, and at intervals between customers, Olivia listened patiently to the woman's life story. Marie had met her husband Caio in France. Being an avid cyclist, he'd gone there on a bicycling vacation, accompanied by a friend. They'd had a stopover one night in Nimes, at the very laubergel Marie's mother and father owned at the time. They'd met in the little bistrot that Marie worked in as a 'serveuse'. After that, they'd kept in touch by post, Caio returning in the summer for a stay. Marie's parents encouraged the relationship almost from the start. Caio seemed like such a nice young man and when they found out his parents were the owners of one of the biggest coffee plantations in Brazil, they were even more enthusiastic. And so it had gone. Eventually there was marriage and a couple of children who were now already a long time married with professional careers, one living right in Fortaleza and the other in Rio de Janeiro.

"I love this little store," the woman said in conclusion, her eyes misting over. "I detest the thought of leaving. I have spent my life here. It is my home. I am sure you understand."

"I do," Olivia said, feeling pangs of sadness. It must be awful, she told herself, to have to leave something you really love.

She went back to her apartment after and sat on the sofa talking to Blaze. "Well, what do you think? Should I buy that business, Blaze, and get ourselves a new place to live?" With his head bopping, the parrot skittered across his perch.

"A new place, Dolly! A new place!"

Olivia chuckled. She felt a great sense of contentment because of what she'd accomplished.

Chapter Three

It didn't take her very long to catch on. In a couple of weeks she felt she could run the business. Marie, she found, was a very good teacher, thorough in every way and offering plenty of tips and 'tricks of the trade'. The most difficult part was arranging shipping for customers. First, of course, there was the special protective packaging and then the postal arrangements. She had never realized before how difficult things could be when goods had to cross borders. She was always grateful whenever a customer decided to take their purchases along with them.

In about five weeks all the papers were signed and in order and Olivia found herself one sunny morning behind the counter all alone and waiting anxiously for her first customer. She'd decided, at least for the time being, to keep the name of the place the same: Things From Brazil. The hand-painted sign on the brick façade, as well as the one hanging out over the sidewalk, advertised the business in four languages, Portuguese, Spanish, English, and French.

In a few days she had the apartment upstairs in just about perfect order. It tended to be hot and stuffy but a couple of window air-conditioners did wonders to cool things down. There were hardwood floors that didn't shine at all, old and clean and as white as bone but seemed just fine as they were. The walls all had fresh paint, in white and lavender, the bathroom in light pink, so there was nothing to be done that way. She hung nice new curtains on the windows, bought a few pieces of less expensive furniture, and picked out some potted plants at a market to give the place some life. Blaze ended up at the window overlooking the busy street and didn't seem out of sorts with the change, adjusting perfectly and remaining every bit as chatty.

One evening, as Olivia climbed the steps to the apartment after a particularly busy day, she realized with chagrin she was going to have to buy a car in order to get heavy things to the post office or to the courier and to pick supplies up too. There just was no other way. She clicked open the door and when Blaze piped up with a prompt "Hello! Hello!" she knew she was home. How far she'd come! she thought with an ecstatic sigh. It was hard for her to believe now that she'd ever worked in any library and gone home day after day to such a loathsome place. Why had she ever put up with things for so long?

Her mother had given up on trying to get her to come back some time ago, but once in a while there were rumblings that way and the issue of health care kept popping up time and time again. It was in every phone conversation. Olivia explained that she was young and healthy and, anyway, she was going to look into some sort of insurance in the near future, not to worry. Brenda, however, was hardly apprehensive. There was never even the slightest intimation on her part that Olivia ought to come back to Canada. In fact there was encouragement for her to stay put. She was quite positive.

"You did right, Olivia," she'd say. "I'm coming down there at Christmas to see you and give you a great bug hug."

Olivia's hair had grown long and she usually wore it just loose, in its natural color without any highlighting or streaks. It was just brown but still it always shone in the store lighting or out in the sun. She looked healthy and natural and years younger than she was. Her face, though having lost some of its deep tan, was still as brown as an acorn, specked with a few freckles. There were hardly any lines around those lovely almond-shaped eyes of hers, amber lights of peace and contentment. At work she dressed well, but not for show, with neatness and a classy sort of plainness being the themes. Nothing she wore in the shop was ever stained or wrinkled, threadbare, or tattered in any way. Her appearance, she knew, would most often be interpreted as a barometer of her integrity. She wore pretty shirts in blue or violet or coral, and cotton slacks, usually in stone or light saddle, with sandals or soft handsewn moccasins for their slipperlike comfort. Her tattered old blue jeans were still a part of her wardrobe and she slipped them on whenever she was out and about, to the market or to the beach or just kicking around the apartment. She saw in them a sign of youth to hold on to.

One day, after a torrential downpour, she saw a new silver Jaguar draw up and park across the street. Most of the cars that she saw down here were Pumas or Opels or Volkswagens. But she was more fascinated by the hazy squiggles of steam that were rising off the glossy street. They reminded her of a soirée for ghosts with the dancing about to commence.

Marius Lane got out of the Jaguar with just one thought in mind: the car suited him and as soon as he got back to Toronto he would look into acquiring one. He locked it, glanced around and, when he saw what he was looking for, strode smartly up the busy sidewalk to the corner, crossing the street at the lights. He looked every bit the tourist and felt sure he stood out. He'd made certain to do himself up well. It wasn't just any old shirt he was wearing but made of the finest silk, short sleeve, in bright red, dappled with just the right number of white lilies; he'd left the first three buttons undone for a glimpse of his chest hair. His black pants were neat and well-pressed, and he watched where he was walking through his dark sunglasses for fear he'd dip into one of the small puddles lying about along the way and throw up nasty little splashes of water onto the gleaming toes of his shoes. His face was pinkish, with not the trace of a tan, as he barely had time to stick his head out the door even in the summer. There lingered on his face a preoccupation.

As he approached the store, he was glad he'd come. He could have stayed away certainly, he knew that, but there never would have been any satisfaction; he would have felt defeated until the day he died. He couldn't let the victory be hers. He walked tall now and, as he was about to enter Things From Brazil, he felt very much like a victorious general about to cut down the last of the enemy.

She was waiting on a customer at the time, a pretty little older woman who wondered what was going on when the transaction came to an abrupt halt. About to take an imprint of the credit card, Olivia froze in disbelief. She couldn't believe her eyes when she saw <u>him</u> step boldly through the doorway. A sinking feeling came over her, as if she'd been dropped from a tower, and then a surge of anger welled up inside her. She felt as if she'd been trespassed upon, her freedom melting like snow in a shower. She clenched her teeth. No, she told herself, I'm not going to let him make me feel this way.

"Why did you come here?" she snapped with a rush of self-confidence. "You know I don't want you here. You know I don't want you at all. You've lost me, don't you know that? You can't always be a winner, no. You've lost this time." She gestured with a victorious wave while the woman at the checkout gaped in bewilderment. "This is mine. This is my business. I own it.

I have my own things now. I have a nice apartment. This is my building. Go home, Marius, and don't ever come back."

He just stood there with a smirk, his arms folded. What a fool she was! he thought. Most, if not all, of the money has come from me. I made it and she spent it. "I could have come sooner," he lied. "I knew where you were. After a week, in fact. I just never thought you were worth pursuing. But I wanted to let you know I could find you. I wasn't going to let you think you'd been successful in eluding me."

"It sounds just like you," she laughed derisively. She wanted to let him know in no uncertain terms just how much she disliked him. "I can't stand you and you know it. And I want you to leave my store. This is my victory, Marius."

At that moment, a young man charged up one of the aisles from the back, where he'd been receiving a shipment of goods. He was in his late twenties, with shorter jet black hair, dark brown eyes, and a distinct jaw line giving him a strong, no nonsense sort of look. He was Spanish and his skin was brown like the leather of a good saddle. Wearing a T-shirt and a pair of jeans, his large chest was well defined and his biceps bulged like balloons. His name was Benito and he didn't seem pleased at all. He stopped at the cash register, clamped his hands on his hips, and stood there glowering at the intruder. Benito was Olivia's helper and he came in now two or three days a week to do some of the heavier work. He had taken quite a liking to her and she was in the process of teaching him English. Marius didn't like the look of this 'Inca', *as* he was thinking of him, and he told himself if it hadn't been for the arrival of the intimidating fellow, he might have hung around longer. He turned with disgust and walked out of the store.

Chapter Four

This wasn't the first time she had come to the beach with Benito, but it was the first good day. She saw only smaller waves coming in quietly and unfurling close in along the shore, where hordes of bathers were frolicking in the jade green water. Benito told her he was going in for a swim and she watched him run off, tacking about between all the blankets, towels, and umbrellas with puffs of sand jumping off the balls of his feet. Reaching the water, he splashed in and then dove like an otter where it got deep enough, slithering out under the crescendo of a wave. Olivia liked the way things were going between them. She lay back and closed her eyes on the sun that was just overhead and watched the black-orange glow on the inside of her eyelids. Benito, she knew, would be happy enough living a spartan existence, as he'd been brought up in the poorest of situations. And she felt that a bit of money for necessities and a little comfort without a lot of frills would be good enough for her as well.

When he came back and sat down beside her, Benito let her know the water was excellent, perfect in temperature and with hardly any currents at all. He took up the newspaper he'd brought along and began to read. It wasn't long before he drew her attention to a good-sized story at the bottom of the front page.

She sat up and read it with extreme interest. Heinrich Von Brauchitsen, Adinaldo's father, had been arrested and charged with crimes from the Second World War. He'd been a high-ranking officer, it said, under Adolf Hitler and had fled Germany after the fall of the Third Reich with his stolen treasures to live out the rest of his life in peace and comfort. The police had confiscated Mr. Von Brauchitsen's extensive collection of paintings and sculptures, and his vast horde of coins, most of them in the form of gold. Adinaldo, the writeup went, had been released on a bond pending further investigation.

Olivia handed the paper back to Benito and sat there with her hands folded in her lap gazing out to sea. She'd figured something was up but now the details were clear. She wondered if the identical twins she'd seen working around the place were Adinaldo's sons. She guessed they were but she'd never know for sure. Partly because of Baldochi, the fisherman, she'd avoided Adinaldo which, as it turned out, had been the right thing to do. She turned and looked into the expectant eyes of her good friend. Benito was staring at her, his mouth open on pearly white teeth, waiting for some kind of reaction from her. There was nothing suspect in his eyes and all she could detect was goodness.

After a moment's reflection, she jumped to her feet and grabbed Benito's hand. "Let's go for a swim," she said, "and after I'll buy us a drink at the bar!"

Benito nodded enthusiastically, his face lighting up, and soon they were walking hand in hand toward the clear warm water that waited for them along the shore.

Chapter Five

Agatha hadn't worked since the summer of the previous year. It was almost eleven by the gold and porcelain clock ticking quietly away on the bedside table and she was still in bed. She had a pounding headache and her eyes, with brownish pouches underneath, were sore to the touch. She had to stop, everybody kept telling her, but it helped her cope with a life that had become, though free of financial problems, humdrum. She luxuriated in the fact that she could lie here in this lovely wide bed the whole day if she wanted, even tomorrow and the day after. The doctor's prognosis, however, was frightening: she wouldn't have to worry about getting old if she kept drinking.

She listened to the thrum of the air-conditioning. She couldn't hear anyone but, given the time, she figured they were more than likely in the rec room. Her stomach was queasy and, feeling hot, she turned down the covers. She could see that it wasn't sunny through the chinks in the blinds. She thought she'd heard rain during the night, hard rain pelting the roof like pebbles. She groaned at the churning in her stomach and knew she was going to be sick. She got out of bed slowly and struggled to the bathroom, her head pounding with each step. Down on her knees in front of the toilet, she lurched forward just in time and spewed out the bitter remains of whatever she'd eaten. She coughed, choking for a second, and then reached for the toilet paper to wipe her nose that dripped and burned with the last dribbles of vomit. She knew it was a special day and would have to rally herself to get things ready. She wriggled into a pair of snug designer blue jeans, pulled a white T-shirt over her head, and at the mirror disentangled her flaxen hair. The comb kept getting stuck and she finally threw it down, grabbing the brush. She ended up drawing the mess into a pony tail and, like an ageing bear, shuffled out of the bedroom.

She could see that they'd all eaten their breakfast, likely ages ago. Natalie would have forced the issue. The table was clear, save for one setting. She gazed out the window and saw a gray, sad day and the river, which was almost black. The grass was wet, and the road too, and water dripped monotonously from somewhere above the window. She turned around wagging her head, wondering what on earth she was doing with her life.

She heard the barely audible sound of music through the wall and it brought a smile to her face. She was the one bright jewel, the light in the night, that little peanut of a Natalie! She hardly felt like eating and sipped hot tea at the table, managing to nibble on a piece of dry toast. How things had changed! she thought. She'd never been a drinker before, not ever, save for a glass of wine now and again when she'd been able to afford it. Grant had done all the drinking and she'd born the brunt of its adverse effects. Now she was the one doling out the poison to others. Such irony! There was too dam little to do and too much time to do it. She needed a goal or a project, something to achieve, not alcohol to help her stymie the monotony. Maybe she ought to join something, a club perhaps or a bowling league in the fall. She wasn't a good mixer, though she did have acquaintances, but they weren't close at all. People she'd met at bingo, merely sprinkles on a cake instead of real icing.

The party was set for four. It was Natalie's first birthday and Agatha had plenty to do in preparation for the little bash. She put her things in the dishwasher and congratulated herself on having kept down the tea and the toast. She turned the dishwasher on, the most expensive one she'd been able to find, and, psychologically at least, felt better. There were benefits to having unlimited funds!

When she stepped into the massive rec room she saw Nathan inching along beside Natalie, holding her tiny hand. He was a very good father even though the child was not his. She had been

worried about that, about him maybe being reproachful with regard to taking on the responsibility. He was making baby talk with the little girl, who was treading unsteadily with a little book in her hand. Natalie liked to pick things up and carry them around. Agatha worried, with those rickety 'petits pas', that she might trip and strike her head on the coffee table or tea wagon or on one of the terra cotta flower pots in which her philodendrons flourished.

As soon as Natalie noticed her she quickened her step, clinging to Nathan's hand.

"Hi, little dear," Agatha said, catching her up in her arms. She kissed her on the cheek, held her for a moment beaming with admiration, and then set her down taking her hand. "Is everyone ready for the big day?...0h, Nathan, the cake will be ready at one and I'll need you to go and pick it up, if you don't mind." Tamara was sitting on the floor in front of the giant TV, leaning back on her hands. "Are you going to take care of the decorations, dear?"

"Yes, mom."

"I'll have a chance to get things going then."

Agatha sat for a time in one of the leather armchairs with Natalie. She was still a bit nauseous but the warm comforting feeling of having a close-knit family somewhat helped her forget. The wisp of a girl nestled in her lap was her pride and joy. Why, they *all* meant so much to her, especially her daughter, who, in a short time, had gone from being a child to a responsible mother, and Nathan too who cared enough to be a good father. She glanced around the lovely and spacious room. Yes, she had everything indeed! The furniture was the best, all leather, well-made, and reflected in the gleaming, dark hardwood floor. She was glad she got help to keep things clean and in order. Tamara, busy enough with Natalie, was nonetheless wonderful that way and, never having had much, was appreciative of the new wealth. There was the TV with its flat movie-theater screen in high definition; there were VCR and DVD players; and players for video games, which both Tamara and Nathan sometimes played for hours. She shook her head in wonder thinking about them clicking the hand controls in such a frenzy. It was just uproarious! She'd finally acquired a collection of art too. There was a painting or a print on every wall in the house, all of them expensive originals. There was no rhyme or reason to them, no one theme. They were just pictures of anything and everything. She did have a weakness however for seascapes and it was somewhat obvious they outnumbered the rest. Glancing into the corner, she saw her Giacometti on its pedestal. Known as 'Large Seated Woman' from 1958 or 1959, the sculpture was a reproduction of the original. His wife Annette had been the model; she was slender, elongated, and had a composed face. Agatha wished she had the talent to be a good artist. She mused that perhaps she ought to open an art shop to occupy her mind. Or even a jewellery store.

The party was a lot of fun, the right thing for a gloomy summer day. The preparations, putting up the decorations and so on had stirred Natalie. She was a wee little thing with wisps of golden hair and Tamara liked to dress her in pink and lace, and white shoes, which took a good scuffing every day. She made sure at night before going to bed that the shoes were whitened and that there was a clean dress ready for morning. Nathan was kept more than busy changing diapers and joked that he couldn't understand where *it* was all coming from. He saw it as his job now, caring for Tamara and the baby. He no longer worked at the store and he didn't know if his unemployment was a temporary thing or not. He was a full-time father, a 'house dad', and he liked it. He was proud of his quick, neat diaper changing, his adeptness at getting the mushy, sopping sponges off cleanly and in a hurry, without a wayward splatter or drip, and getting another on accurately with just the right amount of snugness. He took pride too in feeding his daughter, which was how he referred to her. He had the microwave timings just right. A bottle went in for only so long and then it was shaken. Pasta was easiest and Natalie seemed to love it. The whole job' of baby care was 'a piece of cake' to him. He laughed it off when people declared with a bit of tease that it must be a lot of work. "Hey, you kiddin'? It's my thing. Nothin' to it!" Sitting there just before the party began, he watched his daughter gazing up in wide- eyed awe at the banner gala of decorations strung diagonally in twisting colorful scallops of crêpe paper from corner to corner. There was a soother in her mouth and her large blue eyes rolled like marbles as the drafts of air-conditioning worked their magic and gave life to what otherwise would have been only inanimate adornments. Ball000ns, only in pink, were tied to the furniture, their strings stretched taut as they seemingly tried, like mischievous imps, to break free. A larger, silver balloon broadcasting Happy Birthday and spattered with a motif of tiny pink balloons hovered up above the lamp to which it was tied, teetering one way and another like the lazy head of a giraffe.

Nathan knew things couldn't get any better. He'd 'lucked out' meeting Tamara. It had just been chance, nothing more. And now he had a daughter and, to strengthen the foundation, he wanted to have a baby of his own. He'd not really mentioned it yet, not directly, though he had intimated. It was a little soon after all and then, too, they weren't married. *That,* he was going to get done very soon. Not educated, he was nonetheless hardly lacking in rationale. Where had he to go? Who would hire him other than his father? Oh, there were jobs alright, he could get one sure enough, but for how much? Probably the lowest wage. His standard of living would be nothing like now *This* was princely. Tamara was proud of him for taking up reading and he was glad of his new found ability to express himself in a less guttural way, though he'd be the first to admit there still was a lot of work to do. He'd been thinking too of maybe taking classes at night to obtain his high-school diploma but didn't yet have enough motivation. He was going to be Tamara's husband, was he not? Did his future mother-in-law not have more money than she knew what to do with? He chuckled, thinking how often he'd look at her and imagine money coming out of her ears! Certainly Agatha would not let her family 'do without'. So *there* was a water-tight insurance policy! At times he chided himself for musing about the great fortune. He did love Tamara, it wasn't just about money, not at all. He would have loved her just as much had she not had a wealthy mother or a dime to her name. She was beautiful, she was young—these were the most important things in his eyes—and she was 'nice' too. Pleasant company. Gentle. A terrific mother. Yes, he loved her, there was no question, and life seemed to be a great big bash.

As the birthday party got into full swing—after the ditty was sung and the candles blown out (with Tamara's help)—and everyone was milling about eating cake and ice cream, Tamara looked around and was elated with the turnout. All the people she'd invited had come, even Ethan's better-than-thou parents. She'd felt it her duty to have them.They were, after all, Natalie's paternal grandparents and she could never be selfish enough to prohibit them from playing at least a small part in her daughter's life. They were most appreciative too, fawning over both Natalie and herself like a cat over her kittens. She had the feeling they'd come down a notch to a much more humble and likable pair. They'd brought along a huge box and she could only wonder what was inside. Through one of her friends who'd overheard them talking to someone, Ethan was pretty upset about things. Tamara hardly missed him. He'd made the choice after all, had he not? Certainly he was more refined than Nathan and would acquire a good education, but what he had over Nathan he more than lost in his refusal to accept the responsibility of being a father to his very own daughter.

She was sitting beside Nathan on a sofa and he was spoon-feeding Natalie wee bits of cake and icing and ice cream too and she seemed to be loving it, rarely taking those popping bright eyes of hers off the spoon shuttling back and forth from the dish to her mouth. Taking it all in, Tamara felt most content. She was coddled by both Nathan and her mom and she absolutely loved it. Why, she had time to read, for walks, either alone or with Nathan, and she could pamper herself endlessly. The cabinets were stocked full of the best makeup available, and there were always outings to hairdressers and spas for every imaginable treatment. What more could she possibly hope for?

She went about helping Natalie open her grandparents' gift. It was a bounce and spin zebra and the little girl went wild over it. She clenched her wee fists into rosebuds and shook them in a fit of excitement, bobbing up and down and squealing with delight. Then she stood quite still, examining the zebra, backing up a step and glancing around with a puzzled look on her pie face. Nathan rose and clutched her and her legs raced in the air, coming to an abrupt stop when he set her on the toy. She began bouncing up and down at once with chortles of laughter and then she spun, loving it, screaming for joy, and the guests all roared with laughter. There were gifts of clothes aplenty, pretty little dresses, white and pink stockings, a bonnet or two, pants, and even mittens. She was mesmerized by the toy kitchen that Grant's mother had brought in. There were tears in the woman's eyes as Agatha stood there with her arm around her. Tamara could not help but think how much her father would have loved to be there. He adored children. She was all of a sudden sad and tears welled from her eyes. Though the past was the past, she was still having difficulty believing her father would not come back. Death was not a real thing for her. Despite it happening to people all the time, it held no relative reality as far as she was concerned. Old age and the future were light years away.

Natalie got a set of wood blocks and Tamara could see her daughter was not interested in them. She spent only a minute or so jumbling them up before going back to the zebra, which, Tamara was convinced, would end up being her favorite.

The festivities ended about six and, by half past, everybody was gone. Tamara stood silently at the window with Natalie in her arms and Nathan beside her. She was wistful. She'd been looking forward to the party and now it was over, just like that, a puff of breeze. How time flew! She was glad to see that the clouds were breaking up and that the sun would probably make a showing. She liked to go to the back of the house sometimes to watch the sunsets across the open fields and the woods beyond. What could be more peaceful? she wondered. And weren't sunsets also a sign of hope? "I'll be back again soon," the earth's fiery orange star seemed to be saying, "and there will be another day." That was where hope came from.

She turned to Nathan with a smile and said, "The rain's gone. Let's all of us go for a walk. I've been inside all day and I can hardly stand it."

After dark Agatha lifted the car keys off the hook, opened the back door, and slipped outside. Having had a couple of glasses of wine, she was sedate. She locked the door and walked across the interlocking brick driveway toward the garage. She was ready to do what she'd never done before: drive a car. The thought made her gasp. But she wanted to get away from the computer and buying things. She could hear the crickets in the long, wet grass of the fields and a warm breeze came up to caress her arms and face. She could detect the scents of summer, particularly the clusters of geraniums the gardener had put in to brighten the backyard. There was a hint of the river in the air too, a marine smell, and the feel of lingering humidity from the rain. She noticed, just as she approached the corner of the garage, a narrow swath of fading orange as daylight finally bid adieu.

The garage doors were wide and she didn't think it would be difficult at all backing up. There was actually space enough for three cars, and above the garage, too, there was a loft where anyone could live, with electricity and plumbing and heat too. There was even a made-up bed where the chauffeur/gardener sometimes took a nap in the afternoon. She got in the car quickly, started the motor, and edged out. She knew what to do alright. She'd watched Guy driving the Cadillac enough and it was all just a question of paying attention and obeying the rules of the road. With the remote she closed the garage door and slowly backed around until the car was facing out toward the road, which was a short way down between the rows of vulnerable-looking birch saplings on either side of the lane.

She started away tentatively, glancing this way and that to make sure she wasn't too close to anything and, after what seemed an eternity, she relaxed her grip on the steering wheel and pulled onto the dark road. She was glad not spotting any traffic which would give her a few moments to adjust to the new business of driving. The headlights paved a wonderful wide white path and she kept her eyes on the lines of the road, careful not to go too far left or right. It was easy, she knew it would be, and she sighed with relief. A car soon passed in the opposite direction and then another and, ahead, as she rounded the bend, she kind of froze up at the sight of a cluster of headlights charging towards her. She pleaded with herself to please be calm, keep all eyes ahead, on the lines, not too far this way, not too far that, and not too fast either. When the cars were gone she smiled, relieved, and much more confident. She sat back and drove like an old pro, allowing her thoughts some leeway.

It was a perfect night to get away, as Tamara and Nathan and baby Natalie were off on an overnight visit to a friend's place some forty miles distant and wouldn't be back until tomorrow afternoon. She felt like a poor lost sheep and it was just this, she thought, this loneliness that came around every now and again like a cold dark visitor—this sense of abandonment—that was driving her to drink and have sexual relations with her daughter's boyfriend. God, just the thought seemed horrible enough! What was she doing? It was so darn foolhardy! Didn't she know she'd lose them all—even dear little Natalie—if anyone found out? And word would get around town in a hell of a hurry too! She'd done the rationalizing nevertheless, gone through it to give it justification. She'd explained things to Nathan too, convincing him it was for physical pleasure only, a temporary escape, something to look forward to. He added some fuel to the fire by telling her how much he enjoyed it and didn't mind going on with it—but only if it remained physical. Nothing emotional, not love, no, he wanted to remain faithful 'that way' to her daughter.

When she got to town all the lights seemed overly bright and plentiful. She was on high alert but confident of her driving abilities. She chided herself. What the heck had she been waiting for all this time? Why hadn't she gotten her driver's licence? Didn't she know it wasn't cool not to drive? It was freedom for heaven's sake! God, it was freedom! Riding a wave of elation, she felt the urge for a drink—and soon! Why, she finally had it all! She had the beautiful house, all the amenities that went with it, money galore, a daughter, a grandchild—and even a lover. A terrific lover in fact! Nathan was a good young man.

She made a left on a red light, not paying attention, her thoughts thundering along like a freight train. She heard blaring horns roundabout but hardly paid any attention. No, Nathan was fine. Tamara was lucky to have him. He really wasn't the scoundrel she'd taken him to be in the first place. Not at all. He was compliant and helped her out of her solitude, even if it was only temporarily. The word 'perversion' sometimes came to mind but she paid it little attention. She wasn't going to let herself become too analytical or self-judgmental. It was time for reward and not punishment.

She came to the apartment building where they used to live. The place was a gloomy and repulsive silhouette against the dark sky. She parked at the edge of the lot and stared at it. The illuminated windows reminded her of white checks on a dark cloth, the desperate, hopeful eyes of the poor. Though a peculiar choice for nostaligia, she tried to pinpoint where Grant's car had been when it was towed away. There, she told herself, squinting. There was doubt. She glanced a couple spaces over.

There! There! That was it, she was certain! She felt sheer hopelessness well up inside. She couldn't imagine living here now She pitied the souls who were compelled to pinch pennies as they struggled along. She had to leave. Her imagination was getting the best of her. She sped out of the parking lot, barely missing the fire hydrant, the rear tires of the car thumping off the curb and jarring her. All she wanted to do was flee. She drove recklessly to the old 'hotel'.

Older people often referred to it as a hotel but as far as she knew they did not rent out any rooms. This 'hotel' was merely a place for drinking. She parked on the street, mindless now of who saw her do what. That was one thing she liked about being wealthy: who cared what anyone thought? They could talk all they wanted!

She toted a new handbag, one of six or more, a sleek black Gucci with gold letters and a spaghetti strap. The little 'sack' she used to clutch on her way to work with the few coins inside was gone. As she stepped smartly and with confidence toward the front door of the 'hotel', she could feel her heaviness. She was going to get rid of some weight, soon, somehow. She was big and blond. Her long hair was all combed out, she'd spent time to make sure there was not a tangle, and it shone too in the streetlight like silk. And her jeans were new, deep blue, tight, threatening to break apart at the seat, where her shapely buttocks bulged out like balloons. She was taking on a more mature, middle-aged look and knew it, but she took hope in the fact that losing a few pounds might help her regain some youth. She was not fat, and she was confident she'd not yet reached that line where men would perceive her as such. She dressed alluringly. Tonight, she'd worn a new red halter top to emphasize her large bustline and a gold necklace that seemed to punctuate her cleavage with a bright dangling pearl.

The bar was busy, she knew it would be. It was Saturday and the street was lined with cars. She took note of the couples at the tables. The men at the bar, she remarked with favor, seemed to be gloating at her. She tried to appear demure and inconspicuous as she shuffled up to a stool, her big dark eyes glued on a mirror that said 'Welcome Home' in sprayed-on, snowy white letters. Sitting down, with her purse laced over her bare shoulder where pale freckles had popped out in the summer sun, she cast a cursory look around and caught a number of bolder male eyes stuck on her. She loved it! She was the center of attention, it made all the difference in the world. Wasn't it about time? A shiver of excitement sent tingles all through her. It was titillating to think she had the house all to herself tonight and it didn't look like she was going to have any trouble getting a man to go back there with her.

"A glass of white wine, please," she told the waiter.

He was back in a jiffy, ready to scoop change from his apron purse. But she handed him a five-dollar bill and whisked him away with a flutter of her hand. "All yours," she winked.

Sipping the wine, she could understand how a place like this, though old, dingy, smelling of beer and fried food, could become a second home. Of course, there was the drinking and that was the star attraction. But if a person was feeling lonely, it was just the thing for a temporary fix. They would meet people, the familiar surroundings becoming a kind of home, the usual faces a family. There were televisions in every corner, and she surmised they were on most of the time. They were good company. And the sign by the kitchen said Real Home Cooking, which might be a throwback to childhood and home. A young couple played pool and she gazed at them lethargically, listening to the click-clack of the billiard balls.

After a couple of glasses of wine, and a third set up there in front of her on the bar like a garish jewel, a man sat beside her. He was quite familiar right away and, though she did want to take someone home, she didn't really appreciate the forwardness. Some subtlety would have been better, even if it was hypocritical. The thing was: a less direct, slower process of seduction always seemed to make the end more fulfilling.

"B'Jesus, you're lookin' good!" he exclaimed.

She was taken aback. She looked right at him, detecting the smell of gasoline. Did she know him? Well, she wasn't sure. She had to admit there was an air of familiarity about him. It was his eyes, small fidgety things with a squint. But the full beard was what threw her off. And then it came to her.

"Slim!...Darn, I didn't recognize you! Sure! Sure!"

They shook hands. His calloused, rough palm felt like sandpaper.

"I don't think I ever seen yuh in here before."

"Proabably not," she said, trying to relax. "How's Carol?"

"Carol?" He guffawed and nodded at his half-empty glass of beer. "I wouldn't know for sure. I ain't with her no more, see."

"Oh, I'm sorry to hear," she said honestly. There was a pang in her heart because she'd always thought he loved his wife. But then she was not surprised either. So many marriages just did not last. "You must be quite upset."

"Yup."

He wasn't looking at her and she was sorry now she'd come into the place. She could tell he was going to be hard to get rid of. She felt sorry for him, however, and she was more than willing to lend him an ear, at least for awhile.

"Are you still at the car plant?"

"Yup, I am. B'Jesus, it ain't so busy no more though. A lot o' guys got laid off there not so long ago 'n I don't think the poor buggers'll ever get tuh go back."

"It's a shame," she said flatly.

"The jobs're goin' tuh other countries where things dn get done cheap."

"That's what I've heard."

Out of the corner of her eye, she could see Slim leering at her. There was no way on earth she was taking him home.

"Yuh miss Grant, I bet."

"Yes, I do," she lied.

"Got a boyfriend?" He didn't give her time to answer. "Ah, yuh must have, b'Jesus! A goodlooldn' thing like you! Any guy'd be glad tuh have yuh. Yuh probably got more than one, I bet."

He'd referred to her as a 'thing' and that annoyed her. But she dismissed it in a hurry, realizing where it had come from. He was obviously ignorant and uncouth. "I'm okay that way," she said coolly. "How 'bout me?"

She could smell his sour breath. "I don't think so, Slim. I know Carol and you knew Grant. It just wouldn't seem right somehow. I only came out for a couple drinks, that's all."

He shook his head with a dirty little chuckle and ordered them two more. Then: "I cin show ya a helluva good time, Agatha. We cin go back tuh my place. It's good 'n quiet but I ain't got no air-conditioner. It broke 'n I ain't bothered fixin' it."

"I don't think so, Slim. I really don't," she said with less conviction. She *did* know him, but God, what an unsavory package!

"It's the way I look, ain't it? Hey, I cin wash up, b'Jesus. I bin at work. I'll clean up for yuh. I'll put on somethin' good."

She didn't say no nor did she say yes. They drank for a time, mostly in silence and, looking around, she regretted not having met someone else. There were a couple of handsome men but they might be married or 'attached' and she didn't want to think of herself as a 'housebuster'. At least Slim was single, or so he'd told her. Even then she could not know for sure. The wine was beginning to tell her he might be okay after a shower. It was only going to be the once, she wanted to make that as clear as daylight. No hangers-on, not him anyhow.

He had driven a car but she took him back to her house and he was so surprised by the Cadillac that he said nothing the whole way. She had trouble holding a straight line but made it safely, ending up awkwardly in front of the garage.

"We'll go in here," she said, gesturing at the garage, "in case someone comes home."

She turned on the light and took him up to the loft. "It's over there," she said, pointing to a corner where a shower head drooped like the neck of a goose. "There's soap and shampoo, and a towel on the railing."

Slim was staring at the bed, unmade, messy, the covers turned down in a crumpled heap. "B'Jesus, looks as if someone's beat me to it!"

She smiled at the little joke. "I'll fix it up just right."

She went downstairs and checked that the door was locked. She could already hear the water running. It seemed to fill the garage like a rushing wind. He sure wasn't the 'coolest' man in town but the effects of the wine had lowered her standards. She undressed and waited for him under the covers. It was a bit stifling and she thought she should have opened a window but the air outside was hardly cool either. She turned down the blanket and lay under the sheet. The water finally stopped and the idea that she would soon have a man made her tingle with delight.

"I'm comin'," he said, hurrying to dry himself.

"Don't forget the lights," she told him.

"Don't want 'em on?"

"No."

She couldn't say where all her sex drive was coming from. Her libido seemed to have begun spiralling upwards at thirty-three or -four, creating an almost constant and certainly insatiable desire. She did everything to him a man could possibly want in preparation for the main event, literally driving them both wild. Her face was flushed a deep red and she tingled from head to foot. Though not completely dissatisfied in the end, she was sorry he couldn't have stayed on longer. It *was* usually like that with most of them. But she was not regretful.

She drove him home after without much ado. All the way he kept thanking her effusively and she told him it was okay, she'd enjoyed it a lot. And he hinted that he might want to get together again with her sometime. But she lied and said she was going away for awhile, on a trip to the Far East. She said the Far East only because it happened to come to mind. Maybe, she said, when she got back, she didn't know, she'd see. He was obsessed with the Cadillac and the house too.

"B'Jesus, yuh gotta have a rich old man or somethin'....Or maybe Grant was smarter 'n I reckoned 'n had some big life assurance."

She didn't comment at all.

"Good-bye, Slim," she said, now tiring to the point of irritation.

"Thanks," he told her again. "I won't ever forget!"

She drove home, left the car in front of the garage, and fumbled her way into the house.

It was when she was alone at night that she realized how big the place was. It was actually spooky, and she started at every little noise. She didn't shower but washed with a cloth and used powder with a subtle lily of the valley scent. She got into her big bed and was acutely aware of being all alone. She shivered uneasily even though it was not cold. Her sexual needs had more or less been attended to but she was suddenly down on herself, realizing it more than likely had to do with feelings of loneliness. She knew what she'd done was wrong, morally, but she'd gone ahead and done it anyway, to satisfy an irresistible urge. What had become of her? she wondered. Where had the nice lady gone who used to work at the grocery store? The one who stayed home every night and tended to her little corner of the world like Miss Goody Two Shoes? Why, she'd sunken so low that she picked men up in bars and brought them home to fuck! She was nothing more than a slut. She couldn't even stand the thought. She shuddered and hugged herself under the covers with a horrible feeling of abandonment. She needed a goal of her own, something to achieve, so that in the end she could exclaim with satisfaction, "I've accomplished it!" Oh sure, she was helping Tamara and Nathan along, that was all fine and well and, really, a goal in itself, especially making sure that things went right with Natalie as she was growing up. But it didn't seem enough. There had to be a more personal project of some sort for which to get out of bed in the morning. She closed her eyes on the tears, trying to shut down the machine-gun repetition of the word 'slut' rattling round her mind.

Chapter Six

It was an unusually rainy day for November but still summery warm. Olivia was standing at the front of the store looking out the window at the rain, which was pouring down at an angle, leaving the street glossy and wet. The cars going by left rooster tails of spray in their wake and frothy lines where their tires had gone. Her amber eyes were glazed with fatigue but she was quite attractive nonetheless, neat and trim, and with a coppery face from her occasional days at the beach. She was taking a momentary break from all the bookwork that had come about as a result of internet sales. She could hardly keep up with it anymore and, if not for Benito, his hard work in the packaging department, she didn't know what she would do. The walk-in trade was good but online sales had skyrocketed. She had a website of her own, very professional and all, but most of the business was coming from eBay, where she kept a store and a regular list of items, adding new products from time to time or removing ones that didn't seem to be selling. She was proud of her overwhelming success since striking out on her own and it always made her smile. She was independent, had a tremendous sense of self-worth, and was totally in control of what direction her life took. She owed no one anything.

She turned away from the window and casually walked back through the store, glancing at the shiny handmade dinnerware out on display, at the colorful neat stacks of blankets and sheets, and at the rugs hung up along the wall like great bright flags. It was all hers! This was her shop. And she wouldn't have had it any other way. Just thinking of her life back in Toronto with that miserable man seemed utterly revolting. As she stepped into the small workshop she saw Benito. He was standing there leaning over a box, ready to open it. He was always so good-humored, always seemed to be smiling—such a wonderful change for her! He put down the box cutter and came over. Just looking at him in his jeans and T-shirt, the way he moved, how his muscular body filled out his clothes, aroused her. She loved his swarthy face, his Latin 'visage'—his dark brown eyes and short black hair—and the firm, decisive line of his jaw. They hugged there close to the big open door and she could hear the *rain*

pattering down on the loading dock and in the red gravel of the lot. She could feel the warm caress of a tropical breeze. It was great, this, *her* life, everything about it now She only saw one problem looming on the horizon: Benito had hinted at marriage, at children, too. She'd expected as much, as he was, after all, from an old-time Spanish family. They went to church regularly, fervent banner-bearing Catholics.

His mother even kept all the first Fridays, and of course Holy Days too, and helped the priests out with the washing of the church linen and even did lighter cleaning. Olivia could sense their disapproval over Benito living with her and even Benito's own occasional discontentment about the situation. He had, however, a natural inclination to good humor which made getting around it all so much easier for her. Nonetheless she wasn't, under any circumstances, going to get married to anyone in the near future. They hadn't been through what she had, any of them. Oh, she'd told Benito alright, furnishing details, but even *he* only had a superficial knowledge of her subservient life with Marius. Luckily, she'd not had any children with the rogue? She thought she might with Benito but he seemed to be leaning more toward the marriage thing first and *that* just would not do. She knew he was catching flack from his parents whenever he went over for a visit. They were filling his head full of the popcorn of beliefs and myths from the past—so she believed. At any rate, she'd see. For now she loved him dearly.

They had their lunch there in the back at a crude but clean large table cluttered with bills of laden tacked down with colored rocks. She'd pretty much changed Benito's diet from one rich in red meat to one not so rich, leaning instead more towards vegetables, fish, and poultry. It was hard to wean him completely off meat because he had this 'macho' notion it was good for you and made you big and strong. He particularly liked steak, thick and rare, and whenever he had one, whenever he bought one for himself and brought it home, that was, she'd turn her head, unable to look at the red juices and blood oozing out of the slightly cooked flesh. *Flesh! Imagine!* Why, the word was enough in itself!

She ate up the bean salad she'd made for them earlier, a concoction of her own—dark beans in wine vinegar and olive oil, with chopped onions, red and green pepppers, and a smattering of hot crushed chillies. Benito loved it. And she loved *that* he loved it too, watching him eat it up with gusto. There was whole wheat pits bread to go with it and he soaked up the juices with the sponge of the bread, wiping his plate clean and dry. She left much of the flavorful dressing on her plate in a shallow pool beading with tiny fish eyes of olive oil. This sopping up of juices with bread seemed still to be a somewhat primitive, almost peasant-like practice to her. Perhaps she still carried around a little too much polish and sophistication from her previous life.

They had coffee to drink after, hot and fresh, much tastier than she'd ever had up north and she'd developed a taste for it, using just the right amount of cream to take the edge off it so that it rolled over her tongue smoothly. She considered it to be a health food, and why not? It was grown, it was natural, and there were no additives that she knew of And wasn't cream derived from the milk of a cow?

The rain seemed to be letting up and Benito mentioned going to the beach perhaps later in the week. Olivia was all for it. Her face lit up and her almond-shaped eyes gleamed.

"Thursday!" she said.

"I cannot wait!

His English was coming right along, as she'd been instructing him on a regular basis. On occasion he had to force out words as if they were stuck in his throat, but he was, overall, very good. She guessed that he functioned in this regard at about a grade six or seven level. He did mostly everything in the business too, even some computer work, and it was great when she had to go on errands. He drove too and knew his way around the big bustling city a lot better than she did. The one area, however, where he knew next to nothing, except how to ring in a sale, was the burgeoning coin department.

That was really coming around and she was just so happy about it. Where the rest of the things brought in a good income, the numismatic end of it totally absorbed her interest. She'd come to realize, finally, that 'condition' was everything. There was nothing wrong with owning a 'rare' coin but it was better to own a common coin in a very high grade. She saw coins now as works of art. That was what customers seemed to be indicating with their purchases. For example, a fairly common silver coin in uncirculated condition, with luster and frost and all, and just the right amount and color of patina, would sell much more quickly than a rarer coin in a low grade, one that was dull and gray and worn. So she slanted her coin searches with a view to aesthetics. Local collectors were coming by more and more on a regular basis, mostly looking for Latin American coinage. She was no expert in the area but thanks to her growing library of numismatic books, she was acquiring a better, more workable knowledge. Her field of expertise really was Canadian coins, and thanks to eBay especially and her ads in coin papers, she had visitors come in from the north when the weather started to get miserable up there. The preference, in general, was for crown-sized coins in silver, or gold coins, and this applied to all the collectors who came in, no matter where they were from or their interests. Coin people from the United States loved Morgan silver dollars. And there, again, it was a question of aesthetics. The coins, no matter how common or how many minted, had to be uncirculated, resplendent with cartwheel luster, or have glassy mirror fields with white cameo portraits; and if they had some very attractive patina, especially in sea-green or blue, all the better. She could almost get any price she wanted for them. It was amazing!

The rain stopped and the sun came out and it was hot again. Olivia stayed in the workshop at the back with Benito until the little bell dingled, signalling that someone had come in the store. She tapped Benito on the shoulder and he turned around and they came together for a good long kiss. If it hadn't been for the store, she would have taken him by the hand right at that moment and led him upstairs to make love on their big wide bed.

Thursday came around and they went to the beach in their little white Volkswagen. It had lots of room and was great for picking things up at the post office or at warehouses or for local deliveries as well, very good on gas too, which was important the way the price was going, despite Venezuala's proximity.

It was a breezy day with wind gusts blowing and whipping the sand around in sharp, stinging tails. Olivia saw plenty of tourists on the beach, and cabanas, windbreakers, and big colorful beach umbrellas too. She could invariably pick the tourists out by the milky color of their skin and today, she thought, if they weren't really careful they'd pick up a bad burn. She chose a place there on the hot golden sand not far from a woman with fair skin who'd rented one of the big umbrellas. It looked to be stuck deep enough in the sand but still seemed ready, with each new gust of wind, to take flight, flapping madly and struggling this way and that to free itself like some wild, hogtied animal.

"What do you think, Benito?"

"It is okay," he said.

Benito had worn a speedo, which Olivia considered to be not much more than a male G-string. But she'd gotten used to seeing him in it, and if the truth was known it really did turn her on. It showed much of what he had and it was classy in black, not out of place in Brazil at all, going well with his bronzed, muscular body. She'd caught many women many times giving him the once-over-lightly. She spread out the large beach towel and he set down the couple of good-sized bags they'd brought along with their things. The sun seemed brutal and she said she wanted to go in the water right away to cool off.

She left him there sitting up on the towel, hugging his knees like a sphinx, and soon she was at the frothy shore where the sand was deep brown and smooth as glass from the big waves that came and went. She was glad to get away from the store, and they did this about once every couple of weeks. It was what she liked, not so much the beach and the atmosphere here, but the freedom she enjoyed. She didn't work for anyone, she didn't have to be in any given place at any given time. She was her own boss, master of her own fate. She could come and go as she pleased, and it was wonderful. She closed her eyes and raised her head toward the sun, stretching out her lovely toned arms as if to capture all the goodness of the open air and the tropics that she'd come to love. For the most part, she'd lost many of her old inhibitions. She felt like a stranger still, but among friends, friends who were Brazilian and, at the beach at least, quite exhibitionistic—though not completely on purpose, more out of custom. She'd bought a new bikini in black, a skimpy one, somewhat at Benito's insistence. He told her she was beautiful in it and, in fact, now, as she stood there in the sunshine like a new bronze sculpture, she smiled at the thought that he'd asked her so many times to put it on and model it for him in the apartment. It usually was a prelude to lovemaking.

She went a little further into the warm water there along the shore, until she felt it tickling the top of her calves. The beach was no quiet place. It wasn't so much the tourists who were making the ruckus—albeit a gay and happy one—as the teenageers who came here when they skipped school. They would come in little groups and hang out in bunches like grapes, friendly, harmless, good kids who just wanted to swim and have a good time, escape the tedium and claustrophobia of a classroom. They splashed each other in the water, played water tag, or the boys chased the girls around and the girls would scream in high-pitched falsetto as if they were being somehow threatened. Olivia remembered her own carefree days. She'd been just like them. Though it was only in July and August that she'd gotten to act that way. Here, it would've been all year long! She could smell cigarette smoke and cigars too and it could have been coming from anywhere with the wind the way it was. But when she turned she saw a trio of teenagers, two girls and a boy, smoking at the shoreline. She felt sorry for

them because it would be so hard for them to quit when they got older and started to worry about things like that. For now though, they could do what they wanted; they didn't worry about much, it seemed, except having a good time.

As she stepped out further in the warm water she could see the rougher ocean was stirring up clouds of sand at the bottom. She curled her toes like coils in it to keep from being bowled over. She couldn't help but notice that most of the men were trying to get a good look at her, even as they too tried to stay upright. She didn't mind their eyes as much anymore, taking their salacious stares as compliments. There were few women out in the water, save for some hardy, matronly locals who took bathing as a religion to be practised nearly every day. They had darker skin and didn't really have to worry so much about the sun and its nefarious effects. She swam out a little further but the waves got too powerful and she turned back, trying to ride each frothy whitecap that came along into shore. When she got close enough she pulled back her long brown hair, squeezing out the water, and the skin on her face and arms, in the hot sun, began feeling tight and itchy from the dessicated salt. She tried to pick Benito out as her feet swish-swashed through the last few yards of water where the sand mixed in with the crushed seashells. She couldn't exactly see him in the crowd but there seemed to be a commotion there in the spot where she thought he should have been.

When she came upon the scene his face was contorted in obvious pain and he was massaging his thigh where a welt seemed to be gazing up like a big purplish eye.

"I'm sure sorry," a woman was saying, leaning slightly over him, her hair flopping around like bunches of spaghetti. She was struggling to hold down a big beach umbrella.

Olivia recognized her as the pale 'blond' who'd been there beside them. "They should not rent those things on windy days," she said, trying not to sound overly reproachful. "It's not your fault….Let me take a look, Benito." She crouched to examine his leg. "I'll go and get some ice. At least the skin's not broken."

Without any more ado she jogged off through the sand across the checkerboard of beachgoers, many of whom had sat up to see what was going on. When she got to the mostly deserted patio where the beach bar was, she spotted a waitress heading inside and called out to her. In a moment, she was jogging back with a packet of ice cubes in a dishcloth. Benito, she noted with some displeasure, was happily chatting away with the plump blond.

"Put this on your leg," she said and, looking directly at the woman, told her she would appreciate it if she took the umbrella away. "I just don't think they should rent them on days like this. What if the pole had hit him in the eye?"

The woman didn't say anything and began dragging the umbrella away through the sand. "I am good," said Benito with a nod.

Olivia sat down beside him pouting. She didn't know why she was upset with him. It seemed

silly to get all riled up but she felt threatened and couldn't help it. She wasn't conceited, yet she told herself the woman was hardly any competition, she had not a thing to worry about. Nonetheless, visions of disloyalty and bad memories of her marriage flashed through her mind like dark, haunting slides at a picture show.

"What were you two talking about? It seemed quite cheery."

"Cheery? It is…?"

"Happy. Fun."

"Agatha said she was fearing a burn from the sun. Why she have the umbrella."

"You know her name too," Olivia said with disfavor. But then she was sorry she'd asked him anything at all about the accidental encounter. He was so naïve about things, so juvenile, taking every minute of his life in stride. The way one should, she reasoned now with a smile. "She's friendly. Maybe when she comes back we'll share some of our fruit with her. What d'you think?"

"That would be good."

They kissed and sat together gazing out at the water. An ocean freighter came into view, reminding Olivia of a quiet giant trying to pass unnoticed. It seemed contradictory that anything so big should be so silent.

Agatha was embarrassed by the mishap. She'd drawn everyone's attention and that was about the last thing she wanted to do at the beach. She hadn't gained any more weight, nor had she lost any. She knew what she looked like, especially in a bathing suit, even if it was a one-piece. She was chubby and could feel the straps on her shoulders and the elasticized rings at the top of her legs biting into the fat, pushing out puffy rolls. Plus she was white as snow. She kept her head lowered almost in shame as she dug her way back across the beach. Olivia was sure beautiful, she thought with envy. She had a perfect body and could easily have been a model. She'd noticed many other beautiful women on the beach too and she could not help comparing herself. She just didn't have the drive anymore to improve her looks. Summoning up the will power, getting the right mindset, were the hard parts. Since becoming wealthy she'd become shiftless.

She spread on more sunblock and put on her sunglasses and sat there talking with the couple. "You're not going to get a tan that way," Olivia told her "You surely want to take one north with you....I'm presuming you are from somewhere up there?"

"I sure am."

"I'm from Toronto originally."

"Really?!" Agatha was flabbergasted. "I'm only about eighty miles away. You're Canadian

then?"

"Oh yes."

"On vacation?"

"I live here....With Benito. He's Brazilian; I guess you can tell. We have a business here in Fortaleza."

"What do you do?"

It was hard for them to talk there on the hot beach. The wind was blowing almost steadily, making quite a racket, and the grains of sand flying around were like stinging little needles. People were beginning to leave, but only in dribbles. It was always that way, Olivia thought as she sat there talking to Agatha. The vacationers would hold out the longest, desperate to get their money's worth despite the somewhat unfavorable conditions but the locals, they would stay only briefly, saying hi to their god as it were, and come back for a longer visit on a calmer day. She found Agatha friendly, at the same time sensing her loneliness. While the woman recounted just about everything, she kind of kept an eye on Benito, who was slithering back and forth in the waves like a slippery seal. With the sun shining on his wet back he looked moire. The most amazing thing of all was when Agatha told her she'd won a lottery for more than seven-million dollars.

"I used to play bingo. I still do," she said. "And I go to the casino too, but not very much anymore. Not since my granddaughter was born. I'm the babysitter. It gives Nathan and my daughter a bit of freedom to go to the movies or out to dinner once in a while....As I was saying: I never bought lottery tickets. Then my parents gave me ten for my birthday. One was a winner. I still have to touch myself to believe it."

"You're lucky," Olivia said. "I know what it's like to have money. The downside is you can get pretty darn lazy in a hurry. I was too laid back, I had no drive."

"Yeah, I hear you," Agatha said, with piqued interest. Olivia's words seemed a reflection of her own problems. "I feel exactly like that right now. Exactly. I'm so glad we met."

The next day, in the afternoon, Agatha took a taxi from her hotel to Olivia's store in downtown Fortaleza. She hadn't brought even one pair of shorts, not an oversight, rather because of how she looked in them. She'd brought a couple of pairs of designer jeans and a couple of pairs of twill slacks. She had the khaki twills on but her legs were roasting in the hot sun pouring in through the car windows. The taxi sped along in heavy, noisy traffic with horns bleeping all over the place. She wondered how anyone could stand driving a cab for a living in such a hectic setting. It was simply horrendous. The driver was nice however and didn't seem to mind, keeping his cool and wearing a smile and blathering away in hacked English about this, that, and the other thing. He dropped her off right in front of Things From Brazil and she handed him more than enough reals to make him happy and cause his head to flip up and down as if it had been wound up and couldn't stop. He really was very grateful and she got a vicarious thrill out of the whole thing.

Olivia was busy and Agatha didn't approach her right away, instead roaming around the lovely store, attracted to just about everything. Even the coins that three or four people were poring over in the glass cases as if they were trying to fish the prize out of a goldfish pond. She had some old coins at home and wondered if they were worth anything. They were in a cigar box and they were dark, almost black from lying there so long. But then she didn't care, her thoughts leaping to Nathan like a frog.

He was one of the reasons she'd broken away and come down here. She was becoming too smitten with him. At first she thought she might be able to pull it off, just have him on a casual basis, borrow him as a part time lover. But it wasn't working. When they made love she was reluctant to let him go. She began looking forward right away to the next time with an increasingly heightened sense of anticipation, which was causing her considerable anxiety. Now she had a hankering for Benito. She wanted to make love to him, only once was all, and she hated herself for the obsession. She was not 'bad'. She was a good person, she knew that, and it was a consolation. She really believed it too.

She was standing back a way, admiring one of the rugs on display up on the wall. She thought it might look good there in the rec room in front of her bronze Giacometti. It was large and tan with a maroon border.

"Do you like it?"

She was startled. It was Olivia.

"It's beautiful. I'm going to buy it."

"Would you like to look at a few more before you decide?"

"No. *This* is the one. It'll be fine."

"Okay! ...That was an easy sate! ...I'm going up to the corner for an ice. You can come along if you'd like."

"An ice?"

"You know, the fountain things. Served in a cup and flavored, like ice cream. Like a popsicle, but softer?"

"I guess I wouldn't mind one, it's hot enough today."

"Let me tell Benito."

The patio was roomy, practically stretching all the way out to the curb, allowing just enough room for people to slip by on the sidewalk. They sat as far away from the street as possible, close to the doors of the café, but Agatha could still smell the fumes from the traffic.

"It's pleasant enough but for the cars," Olivia said. "If they never had these yellow umbrellas you wouldn't be able to sit out here on a day such as this….Despite the traffic it's still quite agreeable. I think you appreciate it more if you're inside for any length of time. I hate to say this because it does sound a little contradictory but it really is a breath of fresh air, figuratively speaking."

Instead of ordering an ice, Agatha took a glass of white wine, and thought she saw some disapproval on Olivia's face. She wanted to have wine and that was all there was to it. No one was going to sway her with funny looks or anything else. The wine was chilled and it was good, especially the first two or three sips that cooled the back of her throat. It seemed to her that Olivia was the quiet type, speaking mainly when she had something important to say. She first sipped the strawberry juice with a straw and then scooped up the ice with a tiny silver spoon, all the while hardly uttering a word. Agatha didn't mind as there was plenty going on all around on the busy corner. She watched the cars coming and going until she felt slightly dizzy. The Volkswagens she recognized of course but not the others, strange things that they were. The cacophonous sounds of the big city seemed endless: horns blowing, sirens blaring, tires screeching and squealing, irate drivers—and this she'd not seen before, not to such an extent anyhow—yelling out at other motorists and pedestrians too, on a pretty much nonstop basis. There must have been a church nearby because she heard a bell toll on the hour, scarcely audible over the raging din. She felt the patio itself was a bit crowded, with tourists mostly, and it was obvious because of the way they were dressed: in newer summer clothes, many with bright shopping bags beside their chairs, and cameras on the tables. Ices were the most popular thing. Over in a corner she noticed two handsome young men having glasses of beer. They appeared to be Latinos and the one kept gesturing animatedly about something down the street. Their shoes were black and shiny.

"So what do you think of all of this?" Olivia asked.

"I love it. I really do. I could sit here for hours," Agatha said with a broad smile. "The food here sure smells delicious. I might come back tomorrow for lunch."

"You'd like it."

"Would you stay if I had another glass of wine?"

"Certainly! Benito will do fine. He's very good with numbers, even if his English is a bit unpolished."

The umbrella over their heads was perfectly quiet, the pole not fidgeting at all, the scalloped edges of the parasol only fluttering occasionally in the gentle currents of air.

"Can I buy you a coffee or something?" Agatha wanted to know, feeling mildly uncomfortable sipping wine by herself.

"I suppose. I'll have one, yes."

When the coffee came Agatha asked Olivia how she liked having a residence above a store on such a busy street.

"It's convenient," she explained. "I don't have to drive back and forth to work and I feel good about that. I'm being 'green' and making my contribution to preserving the earth's environment. I'm non-polluting, I guess you could say. It does sound a bit crass when put that way but that's about it. It's economical too. I only have one building to maintain instead of two."

"It makes sense."

"That's the way it was years ago. People who had businesses on what were usually the main street lived above their stores."

"I've never really thought about it." Agatha took a longer drink of wine, leaving only a small pool at the bottom of the glass. "You seem to like it here. I guess you're not going to move back to Canada."

"To visit, nothing more. I have a new life here, and I abhor cold weather."

"Isn't it awful?!"

Olivia leaned back in her chair, her hands laced round her coffee cup. There was an inquisitive but hesitant look on her *face.* "What about you, Agatha?" she said finally. "Now that you have all of that money what are you going to do with the rest of your life?"

"I don't know," Agatha said flatly, and finished her wine. She craved more and glanced nervously around for the waitress.

"Having your own business is very satisfying," Olivia piped up. "Maybe you'd like it."

"I worked in a grocery store," Agatha confessed, feeling her tongue loosening. "I was the produce girl. Little Miss Green Thumb. I made nothing. I hated it. I would never do it again."

When the waitress came round she ordered another glass of wine. "Oh, make it two, would you? The glasses are small."

Olivia smiled only to be polite. It was none of her business if this woman wanted to get drunk here and now She felt sorry for her. There was obviously a lot missing in her life even if she had won a lottery and had all kinds of money.

"You need a goal," she told her assertively, leaning forward now and folding her hands on the table. "The best thing for you would be to own a business."

"I don't know a darn thing about business. I put all that money in the bank—plunk!—and that was it."

"How about a store like mine?"

"I don't know, to tell you the truth."

"Well I've been pondering lately," Olivia went on, "and you may want to hear what I have to
say."

"You're wonderful company, Olivia. I think you're so cool! I envy you and you're strikingly beautiful. You've got it all!"

The wine came and Olivia began having second thoughts. "We can talk about it another time."

"No, speak!" Agatha cajoled. "I'm not drunk. I'm relaxed. I'm enjoying all of this so much. It's been terrific. I'll listen, I promise I will."

The gist of it was that Olivia was thinking of branching out, opening new stores both in Brazil and abroad. That is, selling the rights to use the name 'Things From Brazil' and then supplying the outlets with competitively priced, high-quality products. She would have been the first to admit it had nothing to do with wanting to become wealthy. Though enough money always seemed to come in handy. It was the growth of a personal enterprise that had begun with her purchase of the first store and which she saw as expanding outwards into the world like the roots of a tree. She was successful already and felt great satisfaction at having come so far. But the enterprise was bursting at the seams thanks to the personal computer and the Internet. She saw the potential and embraced it wholeheartedly and one day, perhaps, she would be at the top of a business empire.

"I'm just not content anymore to stop," she said, "and sit on my laurels. The challenge is there and I want to take it up. There can be many more new successes and I want to experience them. You can be a part of this, Agatha. I can show you how. You don't want to just sit around the rest of your life and do nothing. I believe you can accomplish great things both for yourself and for your family. They can all be involved in it."

Agatha was spellbound. She gazed open-mouthed at this beautiful young woman with the earthy looks—the long, shiny brown hair, the tanned face with its sprinkling of freckles, the amber, almond-shaped eyes— and saw, not only contentment, but the epitome of victory over adversity. Olivia had told her all about her life in Toronto with her husband and how she'd escaped—yes, almost like a prisoner!—and come down here to this new freedom and independence and obvious success and satisfaction.

"You're wonderful, Olivia! You're so confident and sure of yourself. You're just so cool!" "Thank-you."

"Oh, for sure. And I'm going to give all of what you said some thought," Agatha told her, pushing aside the empty wine glass and sliding the other one into position. "I know the perfect place for a store. In the casino. Yes!" She'd checked her charm bracelet during Olivia's tirade and seen that the ace of hearts was staring right up at her. "It's a busy place. The only thing would be that maybe people wouldn't have their minds on knives and forks and rugs and all."

"We ship anywhere, Agatha! Surprise gifts or just additions to someone's home. We have collector coins and sets too, don't forget."

"I don't know much about anything like that."

"I'll teach you. The collector sets from the mint usually have a fixed price and they're prepackaged too, in nice little gift box albums. You simply put a price on them."

"And jewellery?"

"A possibility, sure."

In her sudden elation over the new scheme Agatha drank up most of her wine. She took out a kleenex and mopped up the perspiration on her brow and nose. She was very hot and the wine wasn't helping.

"Let's go back to the store," Olivia said. "It's cooler. Besides, Benito might be needing me."

Chapter Seven

It was a hot July day and the sky was completely blue, save for two or three wispy strands of white cloud drifting lazily northward like lost children following one another across a strange land. There was a hot breeze and the dull silvery clusters of artemisia in the flower beds of the vast parking lot seemed to be choking in the desiccated soil that was no more now than fine particles of dust. There were few cars in the lot, perhaps because it was earlier in the week but more likely because of the heat, which shimmered up in blurry waves off the black asphalt. A car trundled along until the driver found what he was looking for in the enormous new plaza that housed dozens of brand-name factory outlet stores. He parked the newer red Ferrari 360 Spider and got out of the air-conditioned car, stepping into the oven of suffocating heat. He was a tallish, well-built man with the look of a retired boxer. His mouth was set into a square jaw and his bushy salt and pepper eyebrows seemed to stick out like ledges over his somewhat deep-set, big blue eyes. There were obvious scars on his ruddy, leathery face—on the side of his broad, crooked nose, his high cheekbone, and another one on his forehead. Despite his pugnacious looks, he had a distinguished, refined appearance, this coming somewhat from his full head of whitish gray hair parted neatly on the side. He was dressed well too. He appeared to be in his late forties or early fifties and his attire was indicative of a businessman who spent his days in an office. He wore a white shirt and sapphire tie and a pair of navy blue slacks pressed perfectly over black buffed shoes. His hands were large, and the first thing anyone noticed was the pav6 diamond watch on his wrist and the large gold ring on his finger.

He locked the car, slipped the keys in his pocket, and strode confidently across the hot asphalt to the store, which was called Things From Brazil.

The young woman inside practically greeted him at the door. She reminded him of a little girl who had prematurely left school out of a sense of rebellion to prove herself in the world of business. She wore no makeup, none that he could see at a glance, and her pale face seemed to be just bordering on womanhood. She was wearing a white dress, cinched at the waist, and it went well with her long black hair. He thought she was very good-looking, modelish was the word that came into his mind, and he found himself wishing, as he often did, that he could be young again and enjoy those glory days once more. Gerard asked her if she had any coin jewellery.

"That sure is a sharp car you have!" she said with a smile, peering past him and out the door. "What is it?"

"A Ferrari," he said in his gravelly voice.

"Wow!"

Gerard got a thrill whenever anyone admired anything of his. It made up, in a sms11 way, for the god-like feeling and all the adulation he'd received during his professional career.

"It's a helluva car. You can get one if you really want one," he said, believing his words. "All you have to do is put your mind to it."

"I wouldn't want to drive it because I'd be afraid of getting in an accident."

"You're not thinking the right way. Hell, you won't get into an accident! You have to be *positive,* young lady."

"I'll show you what we've got. I don't think there's any coin jewellery. I'll ask my mom."

When the young woman slipped through the doorway at the back, Gerard found himself perusing a glass display case full of Canadian and United States coins, all in attractive packaging—but he was hardly interested. He stood up straight, folded his arms on his chest, and looked around. There were blankets and rugs and dinnerware and leather products too, even shoes. It was the leather he could smell and he sniffed at the air like a big bulldog. He loved the smell of leather. It was what greeted him every time he got into the Ferrari, or sat on his chair or his sofa at home. He had a penchant for the finer things in life.

He was soon standing face to face with a woman he guessed to be around forty. She was quite congenial, wanting to shake his hand right away, and she reminded him oddly of vanilla pudding because of her pallor and puffiness. She was a bit overweight, plump, but he appreciated women like that She was blond, which he liked too, and had an ample bust line. He figured she was married.

"I don't have any coin jewellery," she told him. "We specialize in products made in Brazil….There *is* a coin store downtown. They might have something."

"Yeah, I've been there before….I'm staying across the road here," he explained, "and I found your store in the yellow pages under 'Coine."

"We only have these," Agatha said, indicating the display case. "You might look around though and find something else you like.

We have fine leather products at real good prices. Maybe you could surprise your wife with a handmade purse."

"I'm not married and if I had a wife," he laughed, "she'd probably have more purses than she knew what to do with."

Agatha had given him the once-over-lightly and, God, was he ever a hunk! She was already scheming to defer his departure.

"Are you here for the day?"

"I might stay around awhile," he said. "Thought I'd give the car a good run and visit the casino."

"Casino? You like that, do you?"

"Damn right! Great entertainment. Long as you don't get carried away. I don't go for the money anyhow. Just something to do….How about you?"

"Once in a while." Agatha turned to Tamara. "Dear, could you go over and straighten that pile of blankets up for me? The bus we had just went through everything."

Tamara smiled and sauntered away.

"Your daughter?"

"Yes," Agatha said.

"She's pretty."

"She looks a lot like her father."

"Is this your store? Does he work here too?"

"He died."

"Oh… sorry to hear."

Agatha had noticed his ring and scintillating watch. And of course the red sports car. Wow, she thought, nobody would miss that! Her mind was grinding away. She knew she had to hook him somehow before he walked out the door. The business had given her more confidence and really brought out her forwardness. She couldn't hide in a shell if she was to succeed.

"I think I'm going to the casino tonight," she said offhandedly.

He asked her, without hesitating, if she wanted to come along with him for awhile now. "You're not too dam busy. Maybe your daughter can handle it. You'll get to ride in the Ferrari too! How 'bout it?"

"I'll talk to Tamara, just give me a minute."

Agatha, hardly able to contain herself, glided over to where Tamara was refolding and stacking the colorful Brazilian blankets.

"I'm going with him," she said.

"Where?" Tamara was aghast.

"The casino. He invited me. And we're not busy. Nathan will be here soon....We won't be long."

"But you don't know him at all, mom."

"It's only to the casino, dear."

Agatha knew Tamara viewed the man as an intruder in their life, someone who might eventually upset the apple cart and destroy the status quo. She could understand her daughter's remonstrations. Still, she had to be of firm resolve: she had her own life to live as well.

She knew it was a fast car, she could tell just by the look of it and the whine of the motor. She loved the well-dressed cockpit, the leather seats with their red stripes, and the chrome of the shifter that Gerard seemed to cling to as if it had something important to say. The city was busy enough and she expected some sales in the evening when things cooled down. Anyhow, the Internet and eBay always seemed to make up for slow days.

"You're quiet," he said.

"It's just so unexpected. I guess I'm tongue-tied."

"Life should be unpredictable, otherwise there'd be no thrill. I like thrills." He accelerated quickly and she felt herself being pushed back in the seat. "That's what life should be like. You gotta go and get it though."

He was very handsome, no question about it. And she wished she'd worn something a little more sexy, especially up top. She wondered what he was all about. Certainly, many questions were begging for answers. It was this mystery that made a new meeting so interesting, so suspenseful! She shivered at the thought of having him in bed and then chided herself for being unbridled.

The casino was a spectacular place, a mostly glass high-rise with indoor, multi-tiered parking, hundreds of rooms, and dozens of restaurants and shops. As soon as the Ferrari turned the corner and the big red letters at the top googled out, Agatha's heart beat faster and she trembled with anticipation. This was heaven on earth—this man, this car, the casino! It certainly couldn't get any better. She wanted to make the moment last forever.

The casino was a real beehive of activity, complete with bells and horns and whistles. There were people everywhere and those that weren't seated, at a slot machine or a card game or a roulette wheel, seemed to be running amok, hurrying every which way with frenzied looks on their faces as they tried to find treasure somewhere among the thousands of blinking and flashing lights.

Gerard liked his cards and it wasn't long before he was sitting there at a large table playing poker with a cosmopolitan group of people. Agatha knew little about cards, preferring slot machines, and she told him she was "going right over there" to try her luck.

"I'll be here. Till I win," he said, not even turning his head.

She looked at her charm bracelet, and the ace of hearts, facing up, was promising good luck. "You'll win. That's what the charm says."

"Good to know!"

Agatha became absorbed in what she was doing, it was like a drug, and nothing else mattered. She lost thirty dollars at one machine, then went to another and won forty-two. When it seemed to have no more to give, she went down three machines to yet another, where she lost sixty-four. She played one more, hoping with each bet to win, her big tawny eyes mesmerized by the bars and the cherries and the diamonds that kept spinning round and round. It wasn't that she needed money, it was winning that counted. She liked leaving with a sense of satisfaction and a confirmation in her longstanding belief that gewgaws brought luck. As it turned out she won three-hundred and eighty-eight dollars. She whooped for joy. She took her receipt and her purse and got up and hurried over to the poker table to relay the news.

"Great! Hell, that's great, Agatha!" Gerard exclaimed. "One more hand and we'll go 'n celebrate. What d'you say?"

"Yes!...Have you won too?"

"Nope. But it doesn't matter. It's a thrill just the same."

He played and he lost, with a pair of fours. Three aces was hard to beat. He wished everyone at the table good luck and thanked them for the game. Agatha used his cellphone to call the store from the bistrot, where they sat at a little table having drinks.

Tamara answered.

"Is Nathan there?"

"He's coming, mom. I called him."

"How's business?"

"Had a few sales. I'm not rushed off my feet or anything.... When are you coming back?"

"In a while," was all she said.

She wanted to drag things out and was glad that Tamara seemed to have the store in hand. She could daily here for a while. She gave Gerard back his cellphone, wanting to know all about him but not knowing quite how to go about it without seeming overly inquisitive. She liked him. He seemed great fun, and interested so far in the things she liked too.

She looked right into his big blue eyes. "What kind of work do you do?"

He took a long drink of the cold beer, sighing with satisfaction. "Great stuff on a hot day! Hits the spot!…" He was smiling from ear to ear and she could see he had lovely white teeth; they almost didn't look real—so even, so white! "Here, take a look at this." He practically shoved his garish ring in her face. "See what it says?"

"'Stanley Cup Champions'," she read. "You were a hockey player?"

"Yup. And we won the Stanley Cup! And everybody got these rings with the diamonds and the team's insignia and all….Know something?"

"What?"

"Teams have to figure these nuggets into their budgets, believe it or not. They're not cheap!"

"So what do you do now?" she wanted to know, keenly interested. A professional hockey player! Wow, was she impressed! Which explained the car. "Do you work or just travel around looking for fim things to do?"

"I work for myself," he told her. "I love it. I collect coin jewellery and I deal in expensive watches….Here, take a look." He showed her his wristwatch, a work of art. It had a tang case, a pave diamond dial, and a white gold mesh band. "Do you know how much it would sell for?"

"No idea. What kind is it?"

"Patek Philippe."

As they sat drinking in the quiet little bistrot, which was a stark contrast to the cacophony of the casino, Gerard spoke about himself. He was divorced, had been for years, contending that hockey had destroyed his marriage. Away from home much of the time, late night parties, and so on. He had two children.

"Well, not kids anymore, grown-up, married, out on their own." He lived in Toronto, in a condo, right on the lake. "You can see it from Lakeshore Boulevard."

Of course she told him about herself too. The wine was working and she knew she had to be careful of her loose tongue. She didn't want to seem too overt, too easy. She opted for holding a few things back to maintain an aura of mystery. He could be a 'keeper' and she hardly wanted to send him scurrying off. She craved sex with him and waited for some intimation on his part. She didn't tell him about her lottery win, not that she believed he was any con artist, but how could she know? Though he seemed honest enough and open, she knew the cover of a book did not the story tell. She had a family after all and had to be protective, not only of herself but them too.

She found out he didn't mince words. "I've got a nice room in the hotel across from your store. We can go there or get one here."

She was a bit surprised. She wanted him, but was he taking her for granted? She hardly appreciated the precipitousness even if it did open the door. He'd made the first move, all she had to do was provide an answer. She tried to appear calm, collected. "I don't sleep around if that's what you think, Gerard."

"Hell, I didn't mean to offend you, Agatha. I'm goddam sorry if I did. That's how I am. I'm upfront about everything. You're an adult. I'm an adult. I mean, it's what adults do, no? I don't like pussyfooting around, I get right to the point."

"It's alright, I understand," she said, toning down.

There was what seemed to Agatha like a long, enduring silence during which she assessed the situation. She had to face up to it: if she gave in he'd probably become just another number. She wondered what would happen if she said she just wanted to go back to the store. A physical letdown for them both, certainly;

but if that was all there was to him, if that was going to cause him to run off, so be it, she'd be better off. She studied his face when he wasn't looking and he hardly seemed ill-humored. He was glancing around at the ddcor with content and almost naive eyes. It was a romantic, cozy little bar. She liked the rattan chairs and tables with their glass tops, the pastel neons, the ceiling fans that whirred lazily around, and, to absolutely establish a tropical beach theme, the potted palms set about strategically on the antiqued, blond hardwood floor. She had an idea.

"How do you like living by yourself, Gerard?"

He thought for a moment, rubbing his chin, folding his big hands on the table. "Good," he said. "It's good. I don't mind it at all. I can't yell at anyone, there's nobody there. It's taught me to keep my mouth shut even when I get pissed off….It's better for business that way too."

She supposed he didn't like his solitude. She sensed regret, and perhaps frustration. "Let's just get a room right here," she said, and reached across the table, taking his hand.

She began to have doubts about her decision after he'd not called for a week. And after the second week she could feel hope slipping away. In consolation, she reasoned with herself that he must not be worth it, must not be for her, and that, yes, she could definitely do better. On her way out the door one evening early in September, the phone rang. She melted, her heart skipping a beat.

"I've been doing a lot of thinking," he began. "I was lookin' out the window here at all the boats in the lake and it occurred to me how much was gain' on out there and how little in here. I felt like a big man getting small. Not a part of anything anymore…. Why don't you come up, Agatha? Come and see the place. We'll go out for dinner.

"I got some good ideas for business. You might wanna hear about them.... You have to come. I *want* you to come. It's almost an order....Are you still there?"

She was short of breath, so ecstatic was she about the call. She *knew* there had to be a lot more to him. "I'll come, yes!... When?"

Guy, the gardener and sometime chauffeur, drove her to Toronto in the shiny white Cadillac. It was a clear evening, a bit cool, and the traffic seemed to be all going the other way, so they made good time. The high-rise was easy to find, there on the shore of the lake just like he'd said.

Gerard greeted her with a peck on the cheek and took the suitcase from Guy.

"I'll phone and let you know what time Sunday," Agatha told the chauffeur. "Thanks for the

drive."

The first thing Agatha did was open her suitcase and hand Gerard the sheaf of bright blue peacock feathers.

"What the hell are these?" he asked with bulging eyes. He laughed, clutching them out in front of his chest like a trophy.

"They bring good luck," she said. "They worked for mei"

He studied them in disbelief and then glanced around for a place to put them. The good thing, he thought, was that they happened to match the pale gray colors in the living-room. "I know where they're going," he said wisely, as if a light had come on. "Let me take your coat. Have a seat and I'll be right back."

She was relaxing on the sofa when he returned with a lavender vase, which he set down on the hardwood floor beside the armchair. He slipped the feathers in carefully and walked back to stand there beside her.

"Thanks, Agatha. Everybody's gonna have something to talk about now!…Like a coffee? A glass of wine? I bought some wine. For us." He leaned over and kissed her softly on the lips.

Suddenly, nothing mattered to her except the moment. Only Gerard. For all she cared there might not even be a world outside the windows.

He had a mug of beer and she drank wine. He took her on a tour of the place and she could tell everything was the best. The furniture, though plain, had a fine, finished look, and he'd opted for a paint scheme in earth tones, except for the bathroom, which was eggshell white. It was a two-bedroom, with dark hardwood floors, the kitchen having ceramic. The condo had a roomy, open air about it, and Agatha liked it. It was the right size and very free of clutter. Nothing was overdone. The walls had a somewhat abandoned look with only a couple of pictures, which managed nonetheless to really catch the eye. Last, he took her into his pride and joy and she could see what it was right away. The second bedroom was a shrine of memorabilia relating to both his career and his family, with both sharing equal parts. There were trophies galore, from his days in the junior leagues to his glory years in the National Hockey League. He'd been a defenceman, he said, still having managed to score plenty of goals from the blue line with his hard wrist shot; he mimicked one for her and then laughed over it. The trophies were on tables against the wall. There were even some his kids had won, his "boys" as he referred to them, Jacques and Louis. She could see he cared deeply about them, touching their trophies lovingly one by one and lingering in front of their photos too. She was amazed at how much Gerard still looked the way he did way back when, save for his gray hair. He was thorough, there being photos of every important event as his sons grew into men: baptism, first communion, confirmation, graduation from elementary school, high-school, university, stags and does, marriages, births of grandchildren, his sons' days in minor hockey, and so on. He made sure to let her know he was the one hoisting the Stanley Cup.

"Damn, that was a thrill, lemme tell ya!"

They mostly sat around and chatted while boat lights, like white eyes, twinkled and moved on the black pad of the lake. And later on they made love. On Saturday Gerard took her to the hockey game, an exhibition event in which the Toronto Maple Leafs hosted the Phoenix Coyotes. Toronto won. She'd never been to a professional game before and she was astonished to see so many grownups acting like boisterous, unruly kids. Whenever Toronto scored a goal the crowd roared and she thought the roof was going to blow off. Even the seat she was in vibrated like it was charged with electricity. On Sunday they slept in and then made love as the sun poured down its glorious rays on the lake turning it into gold. She made French toast and they ate in bed while the radio prattled quietly in another room. They went out to eat late in the afternoon, at a pasta place not far from the condo that offered the Italian staple in every possible form and with every imaginable sauce, accompanied by just about anything.

Agatha didn't want to leave when Guy came for her. Nor did Grant care to see her go. But she had no choice, she had a business and responsibilities.

"Call me as soon as you get home," he said.

After, Gerard stood at the window gazing out at the lake, which had almost turned black in the fading light. He could still make out the silhouettes of boats moving close in, but those farther out were merely a sprinkling of lights. He smiled, filled with a new happiness. He'd met someone and she was terrific. He recalled many of the things they'd talked about. Agatha definitely was open-minded about business and he considered that an important element for success. She was willing—yes, she was!—to sell coin jewellery and expensive watches. "Those designer things from Switzerland with the fancy French names," she'd called them. She'd told him all about Olivia, how she was "very into coins," and she was certain she'd love the coin jewellery idea and perhaps the watch thing too. He'd been fascinated by Agatha's faith in the computer as a medium for sales. Oh, he had one alright, he'd said, but just for the sake of interest, to pass a little time, not to do business. She'd explained how the worldwide web worked, emphasizing its amazing power to sell things to just about anyone anywhere. He was sold, no question about it. No wonder these young guys, he reflected with a chuckle, were running around everywhere with the things and opening them up, peering at them with goo-goo eyes!

He shoved his hands in his pockets and blinked several times, nibbling on his lip. Though his eyes were turned out the window, he was unseeing, but his mind was working, rolling little snowballs of thought into boulders. Yes, yes! he told himself excitedly: coin jewellery, watches, other things, more stores here, more stores there, more stores everywhere, and franchising worldwide, and a spot too on the stock exchange! Why not? There would be glory again! Not just for him but for them all—just the way it had been the night he and his team had won the Stanley Cup!

The End

CPSIA information can be obtained at www.ICGtesting.com
Printed in the USA
BVOW021539290212

284124BV00001B/51/P

9 781451 257243